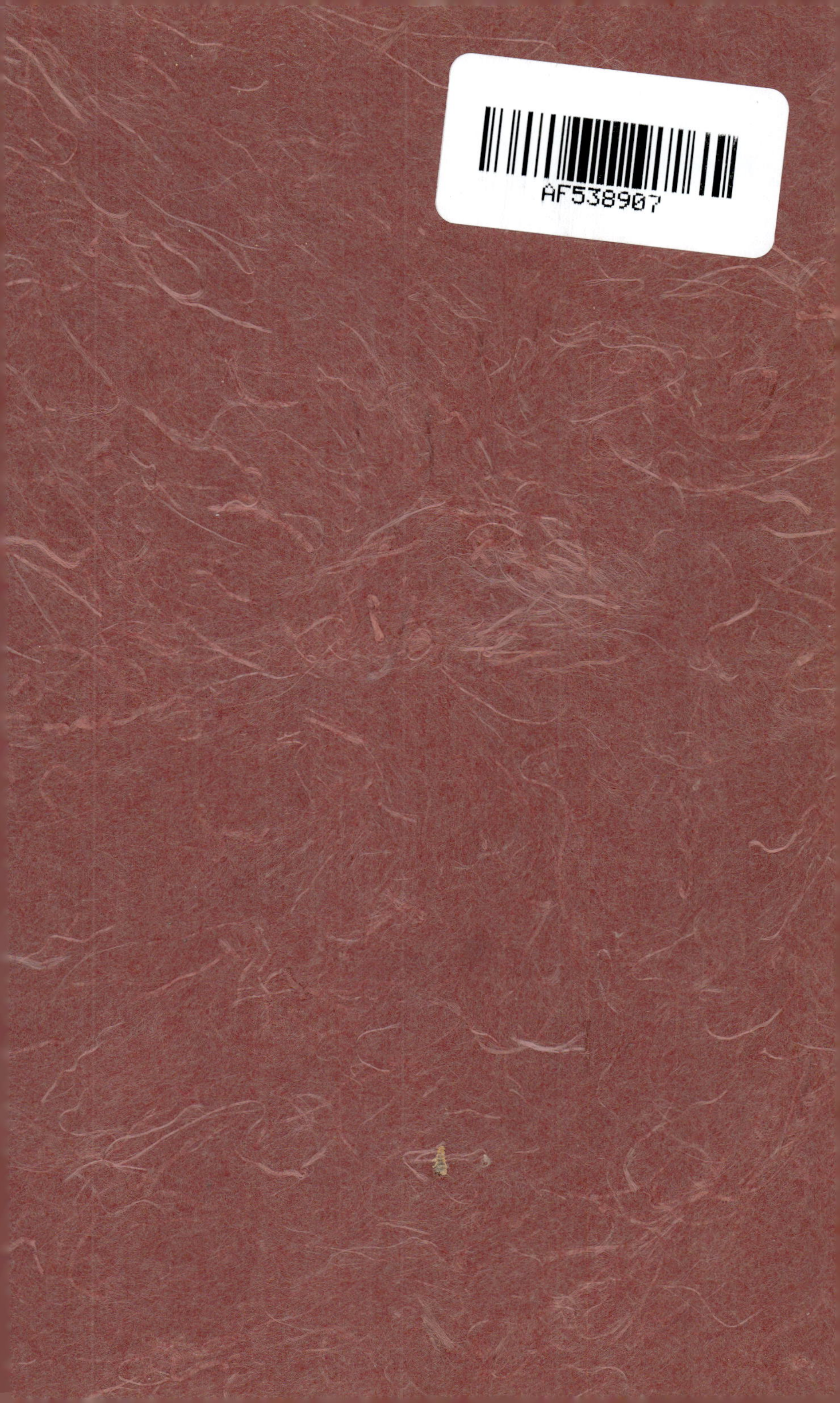
AF538907

Kindred Spirits

Kindred Spirits

Kusum Sawhney

tara press

tara press
(Trade division of India Research Press)
B-4/22, Safdarjung Enclave, New Delhi – 110 029.
Ph.: 24694610; Fax : 24618637
contact@indiaresearchpress.com; bahrisons@vsnl.com
www.indiaresearchpress.com

2005
ISBN : 81-87943- 97- 1

Work of Fictional Writing

Cataloging in Publication Data

KUSUM SAWHNEY
Kindred Spirits
by Kusum Sawhney

1. Fiction - Indian. 2. Contemporary Women 3. Sexuality.
I. Title. II. Author

Printed in India at Focus Impressions, New Delhi – 110 003.

Cover Painting Illustration © Old Fables New Myths by Rekha Rodwittiya
Photo Credit – Prakash Rao
Cover Design ©India Research Press, New Delhi

For my parents

You may write me down in history
with your bitter, twisted lies,
You may trod me in the very dirt
But still, like dust, I'll rise.

Maya Angelou

1

It was raining again. In July it was only natural. But this time it wasn't the usual bulbous showers, the long ceaseless pitter-patter. It wasn't a thin trickle or even the torrential havoc playing monster. It was a combination of all these that continued unabated for days changing so suddenly, we were completely unprepared. Naturally, we all looked like scraggly rats during the monsoon months, trying bravely to hold our own against the watery onslaught.

The roads were full of holes but still it was over – flooded with water which had nowhere to go because the drainage system was so inadequate. Most people cursed each time a car passed by as the driver zoomed past into the numerous puddles unmindful of pedestrians. But the children and dogs loved it. There were groups everywhere.

Inside, the room was teeming with people intent on having a good time. Laughter intermingled with the tinkle of glasses and the hum of voices. In the background, the music had a seductive quality and many were swaying in ecstasy to its beat. Conversations were inane and superficial and those who wanted to indulge in more serious conversations were huddled in small groups away from the loudspeakers, in another world of their own.

Arundhati Diwan sat on the fringe, listening desultorily to the conversation as it flowed from one end to the other.

". . . and he actually told me to leave the house, can

you imagine *that* after all the years I had given his parents and him. . ."

"I have tried the Indian diapers but they are no good. Now I just order them from abroad. Someone or the other from the family keeps going. But I believe there is this place you can order anything and everything from numerous catalogues. Shall we go there tomorrow. . .?"

"We should be proud to be Indians. Today everyone wants to invest in our country. We can now compete with other countries on an equal footing. Our labour is one of the cheapest. . ."

This was spoken by a pint-sized man with an impressive business record who had successfully managed to straddle the country's varying economic policies. Around him were a group of people hanging on to his every word and desperately hoping that by doing so they could become like him. India was changing and most people were excited by the change but it was also catching those who were unprepared in a visceral grip of anxiety, dissatisfaction and turmoil.

"The two P's, poverty and population are the country's undoing. Despite the many steps we take forward we are dragged back two steps because of these insurmountable issues. And there does not seem to be a solution."

In India, thought Arundhati, politics was everywhere. In the food you ate, the house you slept in, the job you did and the friends you made. It concerned everyone and touched everything. It was an amorphous being, something out there that could not be felt. Its influence was all pervasive, and more importantly, intensely personal.

"What a woman, man! What a woman! She's driving me crazy. Just look at her giving me the come on. I can't stand it. Just keep an eye on my wife, while I go and talk to her. . ."

The much-married man was talking about a small slender woman with a cream complexion that owed everything to artifice, sultry lips that enticed men every time she opened her mouth and put on her heavy breathing act and a ready smile that was not always real. Arundhati saw her at several parties.

She giggled constantly which hid a lot about herself and put her on the top list of men who were looking for women of questionable repute. Now she used it to her advantage. In a most charming manner she would begin a sentence correctly only to stop midway in indecision and end up seemingly unsure and confused. Men fell for the act, it made them feel macho and in control.

She opened her heavily painted eyes wide and fluttered her eyelashes. "It's hot," she said. "Could you get me a long cool drink?"

Three eager young men thrust themselves forward with embarrassing speed, one having a slight edge over the other two. "I think I can manage something." His voice was low and suggestive and the implication was not lost on the onlookers.

She smiled knowingly and returned look for look. When he left to get her a drink, she turned her attention to the two slightly downcast admirers fixing one with her eyes and capturing the other by touching his hands lightly.

At parties such as these, one was privy to a variety of scenes, from the ridiculous to the depraved. I watched as a young couple, barely in their teens, enacted their physical preference for each other without a thought for the audience.

They had been eyeing each other the entire evening and after no more than a dozen words felt they were well acquainted.

"This is a great party," she said.

"It's great because you are here," he answered slickly.

"You're just saying that," she pouted knowingly.

"Not at all. You are so amazingly good-looking and sexy. Jesus, what a figure you have."

She snuggled up to him. "That's so sweet of you to say. I think I like you."

Introductions complete, they entered into the next act. They could barely keep their hands off each other and fell kissing against the toilet door. I recoiled from such a public display of intimacy even though it was the norm among the younger generation and marvelled at their gay abandon.

He thrust himself against her almost pushing her to the floor in the process. His hand, which had been hovering on her thigh, now moved up her dress and inside her panties. She, in turn, unzipped his trousers with their obvious bulge and touched his manhood.

"Yes, yes," he said eagerly.

After some heavy grunting, he pushed her down on her knees. She took him in her mouth, sucking enthusiastically, while he closed his eyes in obvious pleasure. He smelt his fingers which were wet with her juices and put his hand in his mouth.

She stood up and put his hand on her breast. With a suddenness that surprised me, he then tore off her panties and pulling her on top of him, both legs astride, her rode her. They climaxed just as another couple walked by with a similar intention on their minds!

Arundhati hated the whole atmosphere not only of the party but of the crowd. It was typical. Men were with their sari- clad wives whom they paid scant attention to as they were busy ogling all the women especially the younger women, who had dressed in skirts and trousers. Why did they look at them as if they were a different species? It was really quite ridiculous. And the woman who got the most attention was wearing a halter top with a sari. She looked good and was decidedly attractive but was being made to feel uncomfortable. It was as if these men had not seen flesh before. They tried to act so suave and refined but it was all a ruse. Their eyes kept darting too and fro in a vain attempt not to be obvious but failing miserably eventually the poor woman had to cover herself with the *pallu* of her sari. You could almost hear an audible sigh of relief from the other women while the men still hovered around her, like bees to honey, hoping for a glimpse of something more.

Arundhati kept to herself as far as it was possible for she found with each successive party she had less and less to say. She enjoyed watching people more than listening to the conversations. Just this morning she had penned a few lines which aptly described the social whirr around her. She had titled it *Cocktail Party:*

All a pretence
All a game
The vanity, the farce
And underneath the pain
The glitter fades
The paint dries
The cookie crumbles
The façade dies.

The words coined by Arundhati seemed particularly appropriate. As the evening wore on, the party took on a surreal quality. Everyone was trying to outdo the other, while becoming more inebriated, desperately attempting to appear controlled but painfully obvious that their attempts were ridiculous. But since they were all in the same state, it hardly seemed to matter. The music soared, the voicesbecame more raucous and the laughter more brittle. Snatches of conversation that whirled past her had little meaning and she knew better than to make sense out of their inanity.

She looked around in horror. She could not believe it, was that an old *jamavar* shawl cut up for upholstery? No, No, it just could not be. She moved forward and touched the sofa reverentially. These people had absolutely no class. The amount of name dropping and the chatting up was quite blatant. Nothing refined about it at all. Everywhere one looked women were in western clothes. It signalled how modern you were, never mind that your midriff tyres and love handles were popping out on all sides. Exotic fruits and vintage wines had been flown in from different parts of the world, while the most expensive chefs in the city had been retained to produce outlandish dishes. Snippets of conversation could be heard about the latest writer. Never mind that no one had actually read the book. But their opinions were expressed convincingly, gleaned from magazines and what others had said before them and that was all that mattered.

She watched a couple who were considered the priest and priestess of high society. They had just dropped in and were already explaining to the hostess that they had come on from another party; had two others to go to and just *had* to make an appearance at the disco.

"Hello darling, what a wonderful party. Everybody seems to be here."

"Well, yes . . . ," said their hostess almost gloatingly. She knew the cream of society was at the party and she revelled in the knowledge that they had all come to "her party!"

". . . .wish we could stay, we are having such a wonderful time but you know how it is. . . ."

"You know how it is," was a favourite phrase used by several people. It seemed to have stretched itself from every conceivable angle and now covered a multitude of emotions.

"Yes I know how it is," said the hostess with a plastic smile. She was grateful they had put in an appearance, that alone would push up her stock in society but she was also upset that they could not stay longer so that more people could see them. She seethed inwardly at what she saw was a kind of betrayal at their decision to go to another party!

A party that was more important than *hers*? It certainly seemed that way if they could only drop by hers but planned to spend the rest of the evening elsewhere. "Whose party are you going to?" she asked almost painfully, trying hard to feign a nonchalant expression.

"The Maliks," they both burst out at the same time. They had been waiting to be asked and once the question was put forward they could not contain themselves. They were trying to act as if they didn't really want to go but according to them their hosts would not survive if they did not put in an appearance. Energetic living and lifestyles were important, and showed you were moving with the times. It did not matter if you looked ridiculous.

Sometimes, she would sit painfully for hours amidst these people lost in her own thoughts and very much alone. She did not have to be so obviously apart from the other women but she had never managed to lose herself with the same abandon as they did in their trite conversations and forced laughter. There was a separateness about her that kept her apart. Others however, misconstrued this distance and saw it as snobbishness.

2

Mina and Shekhar Nair entered the party hands entwined and wit looks of supreme happiness and well-being on their respective faces. It was a big party of about eighty couples, so they had been informed, but did not look that many because of the massive-sized living-room that was flippantly referred to as "the durbar" by friends. Guests had divided themselves into groups depending on matters of business, friendships or plain party talk. It was still the drinking stage and waiters were bustling about doing their best to keep pace with the demand.

Mina looked around her. There were little groups everywhere but it was the women who were more obviously rigid about whom they sat with. To a casual observer they all looked identical; but on closer inspection a definite pattern was discernible. There were three distinct groupings. First and foremost were the housewives who were in the majority. They were usually dressed in silks and chiffons with the standard single-strand pearl necklace or opulent gold jewellery that seemed to give them their much-needed confidence. Conversation veered towards the family, children, recipes, jewellery, clothes and gossip. Then there were the career women who managed to juggle their homes, family and careers successfully. Conversation here was much more high-powered. It revolved around work and the people one met during the course of work, politics and the awareness drive. There was the third group, albeit a small one, which consisted of single career-women who did not think marriage was the ultimate goal along with the peripheral divorcees. There was some intermingling between the second and third groups but not much among the first. They viewed each other with mutual distrust, the former were scared and envious, while the latter turned their noses up against such obvious stagnation.

Mina saw Shilpa, an avid party goer, enter with her husband but he soon vanished to the bar and she knew he would end the evening highly inebriated. She looked stunning in a designer sari made of thin jute and embossed with beads and shells that was part of the designer's stand to demonstrate his affinity with nature, and matching halter top.

Her *pallu* had slipped and we could all see the deep line between her breasts. As she moved her body, they trembled like mounds of jelly. All those who were *au fait*, with the secret devices of fashion, knew she was wearing a wonder bra for her breasts were pushed up high and were threatening to free themselves at any moment. All eyes were riveted on her. The men were salivating, hoping for a glimpse of something more while most women either tittered and spoke in whispers amongst themselves or looked away in embarrassment.

After a few minutes of impasse when nothing happened, Vikas, a complete wastrel and drunk, moved towards her. He walked slowly, so that if someone had known of his intention they could have stopped him. But no one did and to be honest, no one really cared. We all watched fascinated as he walked right up to her and threw the contents of his glass on her blouse. She shrieked in dismay and everyone looked at her to see what was happening. Her blouse was soaking wet and despite being made of jute, completely see-through. We could see the almost non-existent lacy bra, the swell of her breasts and the dark nipples. It was as if she was wearing nothing.

"You stupid oaf, what did you do that for?" she

screamed. Although, her voice was shrill she didn't appear angry nor did her tone suggest anger, rather she seemed to be enjoying the attention. She then threw her almost finished drink back at him, along with the glass which smashed to smithereens on the floor.

Vikas just laughed. He was badly drunk and had no idea of what was happening. She looked around at all the staring faces and shrugged her shoulders emphatically. All this while she did not pull up her *pallu* or drape it around her. No. It was hanging from her waist completely unnoticed amidst the shenanigans that took place.

It was a sordid scene, completely without reason except as a filler between dull moments at high-profile parties. It was reflective of the sham society had become and the depths of depravity people had sunk to. There was nothing to discuss and people were looking for excitement, something base and intrinsically worthless was what kept the adrenalin flowing. Anything dignified and quiet had no meaning.

Arundhati, very much on her own despite being surrounded by other women, smiled warmly when she saw Mina. Mina moved towards her with an affectionate smile but was caught midway by the hostess, who exclaimed loudly in an affected tone: "Is this any time to come, Mina? It is almost eleven and I was thinking of serving dinner....!"

Mrs Sweetie Singh had wide and generous hips, absolutely no waistline and as she moved across the room, one could hear the swish-swish of her thighs as they rubbed against each other despite the very obvious corset she wore to rein them in. Her breasts protuded out in front of her and often they would come in the way when she bent to pick up something. She was wearing a jet black *salwar kameez* because she had heard it had a slimming effect. But unfortunately she could not keep it at that. The embroidery on the *kurta* was a mish-mash of colour and ugly in design so that unfortunately the result of the outfit was to make her look, if anything, larger than she was. Her deep neck-line only served to further emphasise the many number of chins she supported, while the buttons in front of her *salwar* seemed as if they were about to pop off at any moment. As she came forward, the resemblance between a duck and her was not inappropriate!

Mina did not want to tell her that they had deliberately chosen to arrive late, knowing what parties were like. Food would be served after twelve so that it could go on till at least two o'clock. If you could not say your party had continued till the early hours of the morning then it was not worth talking about. Shekhar and she had already eaten and were here just for an hour.

Mina did not have a chance to say anything for the hostess's remark had been heard by others who as if on cue pitched in with their own choice morsels.

"It is still early. The party is just beginning to warm up."

". . . .not really late. My husband came back at ten, had a quick wash and we hurried here."

"Let us enjoy our drinks and then think about food. The night is young and tomorrow is Sunday."

Most of the men and women were enjoying themselves but those ladies swathed in colourful silk saris and weighed down with heavy gold and diamond jewellery, who did not drink and had finished with important gossip, were now ready for their dinner. They could be heard grumbling and as the clock ticked slowly their complaints grew louder and their comments about women who drink more vitriolic.

Mina and Arundhati looked at each other and a shared moment of intimacy passed between them. They had still not met, there were so many people surrounding Mina. Arundhati was used to it and knew it would be another hour before Mina managed to tear herself away from the others.

3

Tara Kapur had made a dramatic entrance earlier with her husband Rohit in tow. Those who had made bets that she could not hold on to him any longer were staring miserably, unhappy at having lost, while the winners were having a whale of a time gloating at the "success of a woman who knows what she wants and goes for it."

Tara looked like a porcelain doll. Most people thought she wouldn't have the nerve to say boo to a goose but underneath that soft exterior, those wide set eyes with long lashes, the trembling lips and small stature, she was tough as old boots as we all discovered when she fought for her husband.

We were all just as surprised as Rohit who went around with a smile on his face and an eagerness that was genuine to be by the side of his wife than with another woman. It was a wonderful change and we were all happy for Tara. She knew she was the centre of attention and savoured the moment of victory with intense pleasure. She shrieked loudly with joy when she saw Arundhati and Mina. They knew it was affected but they understood her need to proclaim her victory to the whole world. They also knew the depth of feeling for them that was underneath the fake display.

There was something different about Tara tonight. There was an intenseness about her, a marked frivolity that was unlike the normally sober and dignified Tara one had come to recognise.

Tara looked around. It was a typical socialite evening. The air was rent with whiffs of various expensive perfumes all competing with each other as were the people who were wearing them. The designer outfits were each more expensive than the other and as to the price tag one could only guess. These were the so-called beautiful people to whom money meant nothing but flowed like the expensive champagne they were drinking.

It was hard work these days, keeping up with the influx of people who had more and more money. They seemed to need to shout it out, to proclaim it to the world. Hence the one upmanship that was constantly taking place. Thus, at parties, ideas became even more bizarre, anything to make a noise, to get the attention of others, to be talked about. For the majority, taste was secondary or never really entered into it. That was not the point at all. What was, was the attention it generated.

Three women were name-dropping shamelessly each in a bid to outdo the other. You may not really know the person you are waxing eloquently about, you may have only seen her somewhere, she might go to the same beauty parlour or even might have been at the same restaurant at the same time. Stories can be woven out of all of this and embellished with enough material to make it appear authentic. After all, in most cases, no one is really going to question you. Most people take it at face value, especially if you name-drop with superb confidence.

"Have you heard," said Mrs Bakshi to Mrs Sood and Dipti Kaintal who were sitting on either side of her, "the latest about Kiran?" Both ladies replied in the negative and then edged closer with great anticipation to hear the "latest".

"Well," said Mrs Bakshi, herself anticipating great pleasure in the telling of the story. "Well, she was seen having lunch with this man. Alone." After a dramatic pause in which both women just stared at her with dilated eyes and open mouths, she added wickedly, "and it's not the first time!"

"How do you know that?" Dipti Kaintal asked the words tumbling out in a torrent. She inched forward almost falling off the chair in her excitement.

"You know Seema, my neighbour, who comes to the kitty once in a while? Well, she saw her once at the Oberoi Hotel coffee-shop with this man in a really cosy situation and then twice my cousin Mala, who also knows her vaguely, saw her in the market shopping with him. He was holding her and and you know what" – she lowered her voice, "he was touching her all over. . . ."

It was more gossip than the ladies had hoped for and they exchanged knowing glances with great gusto. "It is so typical of the woman. She's always got men around her and enjoys them touching her," said Mrs Sood with envy.

Mrs Bakshi moved about in her chair making herself more comfortable. She was ecstatic at being the bearer of such salacious gossip, uncaring if it was true or not. She knew the conversation about this tidbit would go on for quite some time and with her as the bearer of such news, she would be at the centre of attention till the party ended or until some other juicier morsel arrived to rival hers.

All three women were now stuck together as if by birth. Their legs and hands seemed to have come into a life of their own and their voices changed rapidly from loud words to dramatic pauses and hushed whispers.

Being merely rich was no longer enough to grant you instant respect or access to elite circles. One group was talking about holidays. So many people had access to money it was difficult, for instance, to decide where to go for a holiday. One year, Bali and Mauritius might be the place to go and the next year it might even be India. "Getting to know your own country is such a wonderful, wonderful experience," one guest almost cried with enthusiasm. "Yes," piped up another discover India enthusiast; "eating basic food with our hands, with no electricity and minimal water, the *haveli* is a definite must on anyone's agenda."

They were going into raptures and paying phenomenal sums of money to do things the majority of the country had no choice but do and would have gladly invited them to their homes if they knew it would produce this kind of rapt ecstasy!

Another group was flaunting itself by reeling off the names of the clubs they frequented. Being a member of a posh club was *de rigueur* and even within that exclusive group there is a hierarchy of sorts. So, some clubs were better than others depending on the facilities they offered. Five-star clubs where you can say you spent so much on the membership is a thrilling experience. The best is if you can go away to a country-club for a month and talk about it nonchalantly. The bills are enormous and no one really cares. But then that is not the point!

Tara sat down amongst a group of housewives and immediately got involved in the conversation. At any party, she was at ease talking about babies, family problems between in-laws and who was sleeping with whom. Arundhati felt a revulsion against this kind of gossip. She hated talking about people's personal affairs, it was none of their business anyway. Arundhati felt emotionally for the poor, the down-trodden. She believed not enough was being done to alleviate the poverty that was growing like a virus leading to a catalyst of problems that would eventually suffocate them all. It was not someone else's problem but theirs and because of the positions they held in society and the affluence they lived in, they owed it to the poor to better their lot.

Mina, on the other hand, was a mix of the two. She

could adapt to both types of conversations and although she didn't much care for gossip, she managed to curtail her anathema and present the required face. Arundhati, however, was loathe to play-act and made her feelings very obvious.

ARUNDHATI

4

As a child, I had always thought it was important to know the worst of any situation so that you are never taken unawares. Thus I used to think of evil old witches carrying me away and putting me in a pot and boiling me to death, or a dragon breathing great chunks of fire on me and turning me into a baby dragon. My greatest paranoia was that my parents would not recognise me and the sense of abandonment made me sweat in fear.

As I grew older, my fears became more realistic; if I got raped how would I defend myself or what if I was kidnapped and my parents did not give in to the kidnappers' demands? I might be badly mutilated, they might cut off my ear or pull off one of my finger-nails. Those sessions with my kidnappers were real to me and often I would forget I was imagining in my head and let forth great squeals of pain.

The only fear that haunted me as I approached womanhood was that my husband might leave me. Why I should waste my time thinking such thoughts is something I cannot answer. But I would imagine the feeling of emptiness, the shock and pain and would even end up crying in imagined anguish. But despite having prepared myself for the unimaginable, when Avinash left me, it was beyond anything I had ever thought. Nothing could have prepared me for the anger, the absolute blinding fury that he so callously played with my life and then the terrible emptiness that came after there were no more tears to shed and my heart could not entertain any more pain.

I imagined tragedy around every corner and with my fertile imagination I became a willing victim. I was always in danger, the centre of the drama, the heroine without a hero. My dreams never ended with me being rescued, rather I would abruptly terminate them when I saw no one coming to my rescue.

All those years, parts of me were slowly disintegrating and when illusion no longer mattered reality came and devoured the rest.

There was one thing I never acknowledged; how unhappy I was in my marriage. So, when I found myself talking unreservedly without feeling the slightest bit embarrassed or in any way inhibited, I knew I had found true friends.

I had been married for over 20 years into one of the country's leading families. It had been an arranged marriage. My family was royalty, we could trace our ancestors back to three generations. What we didn't have was money but since we had the lineage, the ancestral homes dotted all over the country, the necessary royal connections it was thought to be a "match made in heaven."

My husband and his family, on the other hand, were extremely wealthy. They were one of the premier industrial families in the country and although not considered blue-blooded royalty in the true sense of the word, their vast material wealth made them royalty of another kind.

Everyone said I was the luckiest girl in the world and for a while it certainly felt that way. All my friends were envious and all my relatives suddenly treated me as if I was more than royalty. There was a lot of nudging and winking and good-natured ribbing that is part of a bride-to-be's trousseau. Amidst the general feeling of well-being and festivities, I felt swamped and at times suffocated but when

I tried to express my feelings in words, I was scoffed at. I tried to express my feelings in words, I was scoffed at. After all, I was too young to decide if I was happy or not. Everyone else was, everyone said it was the best alliance possible, so I went along with the general feeling in a bit of a daze.

I was only seventeen.

Like most girls my age, I had grown up on a diet of romance and passion culled English classics such as *Wuthering Heights* and *The King's General*. I would read and re-read these books till I knew each line by heart. Every character was real to me and I would often find myself crying or laughing; one moment plunged in great depths of despair, the next consumed with love or fired with rage. The line had long been crossed and I was no longer just a reader. I was no longer just myself but several different people at different times.

Love for another person that consumed you so completely that you became part of that person was something I desperately craved for. I longed to be enveloped by this emotion; at once so tender like a soft woollen blanked and yet infinitely powerful with a raging intensity, not unlike the fierce rhythms of mother earth. After all, if one had not experienced the agony and ecstasy of love, then one might as well have not lived. I had long decided that the tepid emotions that most people made do as a substitute for love were not for me.

I wanted to fall in love, be in love, live love with an intensity that gave me an ache in my heart and made my pulse race. My head was filled with romantic notions of what my hero would look like. I knew he would be tall with a powerful physique not unlike the Greek gods – Apollo and Zeus. I often imagined this demi-god with a shadowy face sweeping me up in his arms and carrying me across the world. Cave-man tactics appealed to me but I certainly did not want a village idiot or *dehati.* Naturally, this physical side of him would be tempered by outside artefacts, designer clothes and suave manners. Eyes, the reflection of our souls, was also important to me – his would be long-lashed and greeny brown. I think my immense love for my father and brother, both of whom possessed light eyes, had considerable bearing on this particular fantasy.

Created solely from my imagination, this man of my dreams would sweep me off my feet and an almost instant attraction would develop between us according to my fantasy. My heart would be pounding so loudly, I would not be able to hear anything. He would look at me; a deep fathomless look that would sear through my very soul and we would know, deep within us, that we belonged to each other forever.

I had lived the scene so many times it was embedded in my mind, it had become a vital part of my existence and I was only waiting for reality to bring out its inherent mystery and lay bare the smouldering flames.

5

My overactive imagination was given immense succour by Amah, my maid, who had helped bring me into this world and who looked after me as her own.

She was always around, hovering over me like a mother hen, clucking disapproval when I did something wrong, which is the way it is most of the time. I love it when she cradles me in her lap and weaves her magic wand. I love her smell of coconut oil, Nivea cream and jasmine flowers which she always wore in her hair.

Amah had the gift of speech. She could mesmerise with her words and paint pictures and landscapes that transformed me from my bedroom to a magical world outside. The room would be dark but as she spoke, her words dropped little speckles of light that twinkled in the dark and cast a spell over me. The stories were a mixture of the real and imaginary in which wondrous and incredible things happened. I was floating on the magic of her words; sometimes I was a bird flying in the heavens and looking down on the world from high above. Another time I was an ant, almost squashed under a human foot that had no regard for me. I was often a mermaid swimming in the great depths of the sea, the giant whale and dolphin my companions.

I still remember her stories, her voice as it moved in different directions taking on the hue of her character. I never knew where she learnt all these stories but they provided me with another world from where she taught me to see the many layers that exist in what seems just one picture. Her vision enhanced my sense of magic, the belief that it exists and if we want we can make it part of our lives.

Thus, my childhood consisted of magical trips around the globe peopled with almost life-like characters who would wander around my bedroom and let me into their lives. I walked, I ran, I flew and swam from one adventure to another, from the moon to the sun, the wind and sea; they all moved according to my will. I was the fairy queen and my mere thought was their command.

I loved to day-dream. And the best place to do it was at the local temple. I would go with my mother early in the morning and would sit for two whole hours in motionless ecstasy. Soon, I became a regular sight and people thought I must have been a religious person of great standing in my last life!

My mother, however, soon put a stop to all this nonsense. She was a practical woman who knew her daughter's tendency to weave great fantasies and cut my *mandir* visits to a few minutes before school. But I still managed to find time for my day-dreams during the Maths classes that I found incomprehensible and the Sanskrit I found boring.

Despite a persistent belief in the magical and the illusory, I grew up reasonably level-headed. No, don't throw up your hands as if you don't believe me. Just let me finish. I hasten to add as much as one can expect from one whose imaginings dominated her living. My childhood fantasies gave way to romantic notions of a prince upon a horse, there was just a hint of magic as he came galloping towards me. Later on, much later on, in moments of despair, I would see this romanticism as a weakness but after the great tragedy with Avinash try as much as I could, I was unable to completely quash the invasion in my mind of possible magic moments.

How I wish Amah's magical world and its inhabitants were less perfect. I had grown up believing only in the good, anything less than that did not exist. It was a contradiction in a country such as India where so much poverty and disease is rampant but perhaps that was why Amah stuck to the illusory. After all, there was enough unhappiness in the real world. If anyone was foolish it was me for clinging on to fairy tales and despite my ability to imagine the worst, when life had shown its ugly side to me, I had been ill-prepared.

When I opened my heart to my mother and told her how I hoped it would be, she at once admonished me. "These are just stories, make believe. Don't get carried away by all this nonsense. It is much better to find a good man who will look after you." In a moment of confidence, I had let her into my deepest yearnings.

"Mama, can I tell you something, but don't laugh at me," I warned her. I thought she was going to say she was too busy, but then she patted the empty seat next to her and said, "come and tell me."

I talked about my secret hopes, the dreams I had cherished and all that I longed for. "I want to marry someone who is kind and considerate, someone who has a sense of humour, is intelligent without being overbearingly so and a good conversationalist." She rambled on for a time but then looking at her mother's changing face, she ended abruptly. "I just needed to tell you so you know."

"Arundhati, you are living in a dream world, my girl. Wake up to reality. I would be the happiest mother if you could find a man who is everything you have mentioned. But you need to be sensible. If you find a man who is a good and kind person, the rest is not nearly as important or if it is, you can always work on the areas that you feel are important to you. But do not build your hopes up so high. I do not want you to get hurt."

She them looked at the watch and exclaimed, "is that the time? There is so much to do. I have to go," and like the wind, she was gone in a moment.

My mother was an extremely down-to-earth person and immensely practical. It upset me to realise she was almost always right.

If you expect too much, you are always let down. So the best thing to do to protect yourself is never expect too much.

My mother drilled these words into my subconscious a long long time ago. But as is always the case, I did not take her advice but went along with my feeling and expectations and as was inevitable came down with a bang one day wishing as I often did not that I had listened to my mother.

Mrs. Rana, Arundhati's mother, watched from another end of the room. She knew her daughter was suffering. She didn't need to hear the words from her lips to understand the grievous pain that was reflected as sad pools in her eyes.

I had always tried to be brusque with her, to try and undermine the great store she put in her dreams and the belief that only good would happen. I always knew she would go through life experiencing its various emotions, battering against them till she was left supine and exhausted.

I knew when she was to be married my daughter was naïve and innocent and dreamt of a private world where love and passion intermingled and life was an endless tale of madness and an all-consuming torrent of sublime emotions. I was worried for her though I did not show it. Instead, I couched my fears in practical homilies and lectures which she found tedious.

"My dearest child," I would say in moments of despair, "do not depend so much on life, on its fulfilling all the dreams you have about the man you will marry. Try and be sensible."

She would stare at me as if I did not know what I was talking about, as if she had some secret knowledge that assured her of all she wanted. It infuriated me no end and I often wished I could put some sense into her. But all I could do was look on helplessly.

6

Arundhati was unaware of her mother's ruminations. Her eyes were on a personable, self-assured man who was walking across the room. Her mind went back. . . .

My husband-to-be was good looking in a poised kind of way. He was of average height and had unusually light eyes, a ready smile and a quiet confident manner about him.

But the moment I set eyes on him none of the yearned for emotions took place. My heart did not go thump, and I did not feel tongue-tied. My face did not burn and of course the moment our eyes met there was no feeling of overwhelming excitement and desire. I did not feel an ache in my heart, a piercing pain that was part of an intense love. Rather, it was two strangers looking enquiringly at each other and wondering what life had in store for them.

My husband, Avinash, known as Junior to most people, was a pleasant enough man. He spoke well, had a refined manner about him and a gentleness which crept through at odd moments. His position and obvious wealth in society had also given him a certain arrogance. It was not an unkind arrogance, rather it was a mantle that society had given him. His wealth and position in society had allowed him to don that mantle and thus he carried it with an assurance that everything in life could be bought, was within his power to have or to control.

He didn't look me up and down in the infuriating manner most men did when looking for a bride and I liked him for that. He had impeccable manners and though I thought they might be put on, I soon realised they were very much a part of his make up. There was nothing affected or artificial about him and perhaps that is what made me comfortable and I slowly relaxed in his company.

At first there was an awkward silence. I didn't know what to say and he seemed a trifle disconcerted. But he broke the ice by saying, "what a strange situation to be in. You hear about 'arranged meetings' all the time and yet never realise until it happens to you how difficult it is for two people to start chatting as if it was a normal everyday occurrence." I smiled at him in relief and he broke my initial reserve totally when he said with a lovely smile, "what, you too?"

I didn't get to meet him very often after that except when the various wedding functions were taking place. I am myself surprised that I never argued for more time for myself or for us to get to know each other better. "Such a great alliance", "lucky girl" and "what a handsome couple" were refrains that kept me constant companions during those uncertain weeks and echoed loudly each time I voiced my apprehension.

My father was a man of considerable lineage and a generous heart. Coupled with genuine charm and a quick silver tongue he was easy to get along with and thus popular with most people. My mother, on the other hand, was the complete opposite. She was a no nonsense type of person who did not share my father's gift of levity. She was there to scold me, make me do my lessons and give me permission for the do's and don'ts of life. When her mind was made up, nobody could make her budge and when she decided I was to marry Avinash, I knew I had better give in gracefully rather than mope and moan for it was going to happen anyway.

But this was my life, my marriage, so I did make a token

gesture. I felt I was too young to get married.

"I am far too young to get married. I know it is the tradition in our family but I have decided I do not want to follow this particular tradition. It is archaic and obsolete and definitely needs to be put to rest," I burst out angrily with the full force of youth behind me.

"Do you want to study further, map out a career for yourself?" said my mother gently. "No, no. It's just that I am far too young. Shouldn't I finish my undergraduate studies at least?"

"I know you are very young. And in today's world probably more so. You shall do your undergraduate studies after you are married. Indeed it is important that you do so and thus become a valuable asset for your husband in his business dealings. But if there is no other reason then I don't want to refuse such a good match. They don't come again and again. Also there are too many girls and too few boys. I am not going to let this one slip away."

"But . . ."

"Is there someone else you would like to marry? Someone that your father and I do not know about?"

"No."

"Well then don't be silly. After all, I got married when I was sixteen and see how well it has turned out. I think you should talk to your father and see what he has to say." Thus my mother would hear none of it and my father was told to speak to me.

My father understood my fears and apprehensions and although he talked for over an hour, he could not help me to change my mother's mind. He had always been honest and forthright with me.

I wondered if he was talking about himself when he said: "I cannot say I recommend the institution but make sure you marry the right person otherwise life becomes more of a burden than a pleasure." It was hardly the thing to tell a scared seventeen-year-old and with sentiments such as these I got married.

Of course, there was no way this alliance was not going to take place. I knew that. After all, it was not only I who was getting married, it was the joining of two powerful families, each bringing something of great value to the other. It involved other people and their sentiments. I suppose I was just incidental, a pawn in a major shuffle that could benefit many.

I did not have an opportunity to really get to know Avinash and as a dreamer I spent a lot of time wondering what he was like. I built my own picture of him filling in the gaps with what I wanted rather than what was realistic. Thus I went into my marriage with another fantasy where my romantic yearnings would still find succour and the initial cracks were plastered with other dreams.

These thoughts prevented me from seeing him as he was and I lived those days in hazy bliss, in mind-filled solitude, on the periphery of reality while all around me the wedding preparations went on. But they did not pierce the cocoon I had surrounded myself in and in a sense I became an onlooker in my own wedding, the most dramatic event of my life.

It is true when they say that sometimes the most important events in your life don't impinge on your mind, don't make themselves known till it is too late.

7

Rusi Chinoy, an elderly gentleman who owned one of the oldest bookshops in the city, The Nest, was trying to catch Arundhati's attention.

She smiled in response and waved gently. She liked him. He was one of a dying breed of men, who were courteous and whose language and conversation was filled with old world witticisms and enjoyable anecdotes. She felt invigorated by his quick repartees and intelligent observations, it was such a refreshing change. She also enjoyed browsing in his bookshop which was slowly and inevitably losing out to the major league bookstores, that were sprouting up all over the country, backed by big money and catchy advertising.

The drawing room was beginning to fill up as more guests arrived. There was much activity as waiters and car attendants rushed to and fro in an attempt to keep up with the influx. Arundhati looked around her.

The house was simply exquisite. It was a huge house built along the lines of the old Elizabethan manors in England. There was plenty of teak in superb condition and a majestic fireplace which looked splendid when lit on cold winter nights. It was an unusual feature in the house and had pride of place in the drawing room. The Persian carpet was obviously an antique as were most of the other pieces artfully displayed around the house. In the lobby was a truly awe-inspiring staircase that left most people gaping at its beauty. It was hand-carved by master craftsmen who had painstakingly created a work of art and made a splendid backdrop to the stained glass windows that was parallel to the stairs. There was a lot of glass through which one could see the huge expanse of land. Acre upon acre of luscious greenery teeming with a mind-boggling array of blooming flowers.

Arundhati looked at the road across the house. She could just see it through the tiny gaps in the design of the cemented boundary wall and the leafy growth. A huge festering rubbish dump had established itself looked incongruous against the palatial houses. There was a cow contentedly chewing his dinner, while a beggar rummaged through the rubbish hoping to find either something to eat or something of value he could hawk. A group of children, totally oblivious to the mound of dirt, played amidst the heap, picking up bits of rubbish and throwing it at each other.

It was as though the dump had a life of its own. It beckoned and those who knew its potential found their livelihood, sustenance and play in its confines. It represented the immense fortitude of people.

We all lived with this poverty. We became immune to the filth, the destitution and the increasing grime because although it surrounded us we had created a distance by surrounding ourselves with beautiful things. In a sense, it didn't touch us and thus we thought ourselves immune.

The rich were different. You could see it in their lifestyles, the big houses and even bigger gardens, the bevy of servants who appeared with the mere flick of a finger or a slight turn of the head. The fleet of shining cars outside the driveway that enveloped you in luxury, so you moved from one place to another in relative comfort. You looked outside but hardly saw the teeming millions, the poor, the miserable. It was not your fault, you only recognised your own kind.

Arundhati was fed up of it all. The glitz, the unreal lives. All so far removed from ordinary living, the day-to-day existence of the poor. When she was young, it had all seemed so fairy-like but now there seemed to be a hidden menace in everything with shadows crouching everywhere. The kind of wealth displayed upset her now. It seemed so shameless and insensitive. It wasn't that she didn't enjoy her creature comforts because she did but did one have to flaunt it in such an obvious manner?

In India anyone with any kind of money would not dream of being seen in a three-wheeler scooter or rickshaw. It just is not done. If you are fabulously wealthy, then you have an imported car; a BMW, a Mercedes, or Jaguar. If you do not fall in the category well you make do with the slightly cheaper imported limousines such as Toyota Camry, Hyundai or Honda. Then of course there are the local cars, a Ford, Tata Sumo or Maruti 1000 which means you are doing well. The profusion of Marutis on the road said a lot for India's burgeoning middle class as it did for the car industry. . . .

In Indian society, the car ruled supreme. The rickshaw, cycles and scooters that were the common man's lot were looked upon with disdain. They were inferior modes of transport and could never match the haloed status of the four horse-power engined vehicle. The pedestrian is not unlike the animals who roam the street, shunted from place to place by a more powerful force. He is dismissed scathingly for he does nothing but disrupt the smooth purring speed of the car that moves with undulating sensuality, knowing it is the king of them all.

Arundhati had never sat in anything but the best. As far back as she could remember it had always been one foreign car or the other. Nowadays it was, the new Maybach Mercedes, a stallion of a car and worth every crore spent on it! She took it all for granted. It was not that she actively thought about which car to buy or which to be driven in. Those choices had never had to be made. Everything had always been laid out for her.

She was thirty-six and an aristocrat in her own right. Whenever she stepped out of the car, a few admiring glances came her way both for the car and for herself. She had always been admired and was one of the most photographed women in the country. Almost every magazine had done one feature or the other on her from the time she was a toddler. But she barely acknowledged the looks around her. She had been brought up to believe that restraint in everything was essential and did not allow herself to smile much though she would have loved to.

Arundhati was beautiful. There was no other way to describe her. Her jet black hair almost reached her waist and no matter the amount of effort, she usually left it flowing except on those very hot days when she put it into a chignon. She was tall for an Indian woman, five feet eleven inches in her bare feet and with her shoes on, at least two inch heels she was quite something. It had as much to do with her innate beauty as with her own distinctive sense of style. Her peach and white cotton sari might have seemed a trifle ordinary on someone else, but worn with the enormous solitaire earrings and matching bracelet, she appeared very much the wealthy *soignee* society lady.

Despite being one of the most public figures of the city, she had somehow managed to escape. Part of her charm came from her reticence, from a sense one had of something withheld. That was the essence of her; the mystique of reticence. And that is why people gossiped about her even more.

Arundhati could not remember a time when she had actually

enjoyed herself. It was the same plastic event. Everyone trying to outdo the other with their clothes, and it wasn't a trait that women exhibited solely, men had also entered this domain with their Cartier watches and Dunhill jackets. At that very moment she passed a group discussing Gucci shoes and Versace suits. In another group a very obvious attempt at flattery was going on between two women. The recipient was a wealthy diamond merchant's wife who lapped it up as her due. 'God, spare me', Arundhati thought to herself. She had enough of all this. She moved towards the balcony.

I sit amidst the luxurious confines of the garden swing letting the cool wafts of air envelope me from the cooler. A rickshaw wallah pulled up outside the gate. He was bathed in sweat that shone on his near naked body like drops of crystal. His face was puffed, from the gruelling exertion and exacerbated by the humidity which was stifling. His mouth was wide open trying to breathe in air too quickly. He was a small fellow with more bone than flesh and seemed totally unsuited to carry the enormous weight of his rickshaw and the three passengers who sat atop it.

As he turned the corner, he mustered all his strength and pulled the rickshaw forward. He had to negogiate with difficulty for the turn was narrow and he barely managed to keep his vehicle and its passengers from tilting over. Having regained his balance, he stopped for what must have been half a second but no more for the madam was already arguing with him.

I wondered what she was saying. No doubt she was complaining about the rain and wet mud, the bumpiness of the road due to the many pot holes and the ineffectualness of the rickshaw to protect her from it all. She blamed it all on the poor man and he was powerless to retaliate in face of the verbal onslaught.

I walked to the back of the house and saw the *dhobi ghats* on the right inescapable with the white sheets, shirts, trousers, *kurtas* and other clothes hanging out to dry in their hundreds. I watched the washerwoman scrubbing the clothes and wondered why people did not care that their clothes were being inadequately cleaned. Bundled together, from hospitals or kitchens, babies nappies, kurtas, saris and soiled napkins, what protection did they have against each other? After that they were then washed in water that was hardly definable as clean. It was a superficial cleanliness that was a reflection of a society that was individually clean but collectively dirty.

Nearby the children were playing together and every now and then they would splash into that same water. While both man and beast would come and drink, others would spit or blow their noses. A child came towards the water and urinated close by.

She could hear the strains of music from afar. The thunder of drums and the blaring trumpets that fell and rose to the rhythm of popular movie songs. Somewhere, someone was getting married. . . .

After the marriage ceremony, I was driven to my new home in a convertible silver grey Rolls-Royce imported specially for the wedding. It was beautifully decorated with white and pink roses and matching gladioli and was unusually strung together with pure silver chains. In the car apart from the driver, was my husband, his sister, another cousin and of course me. My mother-in-law had already gone on ahead to welcome me to my new home.

At the house I was received with garlands of perfumed roses in all the different shades; red, white, peach and pink. No other garland had ever looked so beautiful. You could hardly see my face, there were so many garlands on my neck. Someone, I don't exactly remember who rescued me from my flowery burden and I managed to walk inside the house. The portals of the house, carved intricately by a master craftsman and standing with great pride, were invitingly strung with row upon row of jasmine,marigold and gladioli. The beige granite floor was barely visible and was decroated with red, yellow and green patterns that beckoned invitingly and with a feeling of well-being I waited to take my first steps inside my new home.

My mother-in-law was waiting with a silver *thaali* in her hand. She poured some oil on the floor on either side of my feet and then asked me to sip the milk filled with rose petals, from the tray. All the while the women of the house were chanting prayers invoking God's blessings for a prosperous and happy marriage. It was an emotional moment and I felt my eyes fill with tears of happiness. I vowed to make my marriage a happy one and be a devoted daughter-in-law. Thus armed with blessings and protected from evil, I took my first steps in my new home.

With such a propitious beginning, I could hardly conceive that things would not go well.

8

Life for Arundhati in her new home was different. Here the news on the radio was turned on early in the morning by her father-in-law and its sound penetrated through the walls of her room and her slumbering senses. The television was switched on for good quality programmes, like *The World This Week* and the *CNN* news. During the day opera music reveberated through the house and she soon learnt the different concertos and even began to enjoy them.

There were magazines and journals lying around that she never knew existed and row after row of books in the library. They were bulging on all sides; voluminous stacks with their dark leather binding and impressive gold titles.

All the great works could be found here, Shakespeare, Coleridge, Aristotle, Confucius; The list was endless. There were also the modern writers such as Achebe, Gordimer, Naipaul, Garcia Marquez and Rushdie.

She particularly enjoyed the South African writer, Nadine Gordimer's classic short story *Some Monday for Sure.* It spoke volumes to her about the different types of suffering and yet. . .the resilience of human beings. . . their immense capacity to both give and take. . . love, compassion and devotion were part of their great positives while those same human beings could be cruel, evil and even inhuman. The story painted a dismal picture of life and yet as the title suggested conveyed great hope. In the face of the gargantuan changes that had taken place in South Africa in the recent past it was as the author had prophesied and her prophecy had indeed come true. For *Some Monday for Sure* had surely come about.

The library became her saviour and later on her friend. She would spend hours just gazing in rapt wonder and gently leafing through the pages taking her far away into a private world.

Each day spent browsing in the library brought different perspectives and opened new vistas. Always fond of reading, the library and its books became her new friends. This tentative friendship blossomed as she found herself left increasingly alone. And once again, she inhabited a world that was beyond the present, where new influences and new thoughts brought a greater depth and luminosity. It was not unlike burrowing herself in Amah's fairy tales but now there was a sharper focus and a deeper understanding. She knew she was consciously escaping to places where she buried her pain and forgot who she was.

Meals were quiet affairs where a lot of eye contact was made but words were used sparingly. You were studied and judged through your actions without a word spoken. The clatter of a fork dropped by mistake would reveberate through the house like the sound of beating drums. Napkins were used to dab at painted lips, throats were cleared often but full-throated laughter was a rarity although a well-modulated tinkle was heard once in a while.

It was a different life from the one she was born into. The pace was slower. In her parents' house, there was always noise in the air. There were so many varied sounds reveberating simultaneously. The early morning *ragas* blended in with the unending cries for tea. The fragrance of lingering incense and piping hot *paranthas* coincided with being pampered by Amah while simultaneously you could hear her mother's arguments with the cook. The silence in the afternoon and the quiet footsteps of the squirrels in the garden went together with lethargy that could only be dispelled by several cups of tea. The warm *samosas* and fresh *dhokla* merely whetted the appetite before the main event, the evening meal. Here great mounds of food were wolfed down amidst the silver *thaalis* and crisp white linen, the noise of mingled voices and laughter.

Arundhati, a quiet and reserved person, drew succour from the laughter and noise that seemed to overflow like a gushing waterfall from her parents' house. In her new home, without the noisy backdrop, she became more quiet. She moved soundlessly and could merge into the walls or disappear into the design of the carpet with complete ease. She learnt to do things without attracting attention to herself, so you often forgot she was there.

She loved the house. The great square patterned walnut door with enormous brass knobs that were neither round nor square nor oval but fitted just right into the palm of your hand and opened into the sun-filled hallway with bevilled glass windows and enormous palm and date trees. There was a small pond inside filled with a variety of fish to make it interesting and it also provided an air of coolness and tranquillity that was very Mediterranean.

Arundhati and Avinash have a large room with a combined dressing room and *en suite* bathroom. The room looks larger than it is as a result of the huge glass windows everywhere which provide me a perfect view of the garden. It is blooming with all kinds of flowers. But my favourites are the gladioli, dignified in all their doverse hues and the sweet smelling jasmine that perfumes my balcony. There are plenty of old trees but pride of place goes to the banyan tree which is hundreds of years old and stands guard over us all. I have often been soothed by its dark cool confines, taken succour from its deep-rooted presence. It has been a friend to me through my travails, witnessing my initial awkwardness and helping me to grow from promise into a full-grown sapling.

The other bedroom which I frequent almost as much as my own is my father-in-law's. My in-laws slept separately long before I entered the house. His room is disorganised and cluttered with newspapers, magazines and books which line the wall. He is a voracious reader and loves nothing better than to discuss some item in the paper or a novel that he has just read.

We become close as a result of the long hours we spend together, a sense of companionship is forged though no real secrets are ever shared. He can talk for hours and I am a good listener, for I have perfected the art of appearing to be enrapt by what he says, while all the while I am busy with my own thoughts. Now and then when I break from my ruminations, I see a slight bespectacled man, with drooping shoulders and a soft expression. He is distinguished looking with his grey hair and gentle eyes. His hands are always in the air giving added credence to what he says.

His wife has no time for him and looks on in amusement when she finds us together. But it was his non-prejudicial look that helped me in my early days and his constant words of welcome: "Why hello, Arundhati. Come and listen to this new record I bought today," that saw me through the early days when I was caught in the nether world; between my mother's home and my new house.

I came here to escape from the undercurrents that were part of a house where two women have to coexist together. His room was neutral ground and neither of us brought our problems here. Just once, very early on, I was visibly upset over some small issue and he saw what my face could not hide. Then that once he transgressed the hidden line. He looked at me with genuine concern and took my trembling hands in his. With true sincerity he said, "you are the *bahu* of this house, you are the new wind that brings with it many changes. The old inhabitants must learn to adapt, learn to coexist together. By giving completely and generously, we will be able to make a go of it."

I stared at him in gratitude and wished I could say something equally beautiful but before I could speak, he withdrew as if he had already said too much. He retreated tp a safer subject and the one moment of real intimacy was gone forever.

He died suddenly while reading one of his favourite books. One moment he was there, rocking in his favourite chair, cocking his ear to a particular strain of music, talking with his arms akimbo, while all the while his soft smile never wavered.

I grieve for him in solitude for not even Avinash can understand my pain, "He was my father, Arundhati and even I have dealt with the pain." The reference being that if he had put away his grief so should I, for I had only known him a few years. In that moment, I hate him for making a mockery of my feeling and take out my frustration on the banyan tree. I pummel it with my fists, shout out expecting any moment to be answered and treat it to a fair amount of abuse. It remains as steadfast and impassive as ever and finally having drained myself emotionally and wrung out the aches and pain, I return to the household spent but at peace with myself.

Arundhati's mother-in-law was inconsolable. Her husband of over forty years had left her without any warning. She felt it was really most inconsiderate of him. He could have given her a hint, some indication. His death left her totally unprepared and her incredulity that he could do such a thing without letting her in on the act acted as a shield in those first few days and protected her from her growing sorrow.

She recalled all his good qualities; his kindness, his amiable nature and soft-spoken words, his dependability. All those characteristics that used to irritate her when he was alive. She yearned for his recumbent form at night. They hardly ever spoke but there was a companionship built on those forty years that kept them company. She found herself lying awake at night staring at the ceiling though longing for sleep. She had hated his snoring and loud mutterings which could be heard in her room and she would often get up to kick him or pinch his nostrils together. She felt empty.

Her daughter-in-law, herself grieving, tried to be sympathetic and would sit with her from time to time. She was a good girl but she did not need her pity.

She went into his study and looked at the books and magazines lying everywhere gathering dust and looking curiously bereft. There was a packet of half-finished cigarettes lying on the table and some Vicks tablets waiting to be used. The record-player still had the last album he was listening to and she wondered how it was still on the turntable. He was meticulous about putting the records back in their covers. Then she remembered he must have been listening to the music when he had his attack. She was suddenly afraid of being alone. She sat down in his rocking chair and let go of the tears that had been hovering on the surface.

A vein began to pulse on her temple and she gave in to the instinct to rub it gently with her fingers.

9

Once the euphoria had settled, I had my first brush with reality.

Married at seventeen, I still had some growing up to do. I had thought as I am sure my mother did, that the younger a girl was when she got married, the easier it would be for her to adapt to her new home. Somehow that never worked with me.

Needless to say life never came anyway close to the rosy expectations I had imbued it with.

My husband burned out to be the most complex and reserved of individuals. Every time I tried to get close he would withdraw even further and cocoon himself in veils of politeness and a kind of *noblesse oblige* that left me bewildered and hurt. I was young and had much to learn in terms of etiquette. I was forever being indiscreet and demonstrating my openness. If anything, this made my husband withdraw even further into any number of chosen facades so that my spontaneity and demonstrativeness soon sapped in the face of his enigmatic behaviour.

At first, I made many mistakes thinking his reserve could be broken. I would push myself upon him and try and hug him as much as possible. But gradually with dreadful disquiet, I realised he did not like being touched by me. It was as if I repelled him. But how can that be, I thought, he had married me, hadn't he? He was much older than myself, he could have decided he did not want me and no one would have thought anything of it. What did he have to hide? Love is such simple word to say and such a complex word to define. It carries a multitude of emotions, none of which are easy to understand.

Avinash and I talk in the evenings when he comes home from work. We sit in the balcony outside our bedroom with the view of the lawn stretching out in luscious abandon before us. I enjoy these moments of complete privacy.

We talk about inconsequentials. Avinash always asks me how my day has been. "Did you have a good day?" or "what did you do today?" are frequent questions and usually sets the tone for the evening. He tells me about the business deals he is doing, the people involved, the entertaining that needs to be done, if I will oblige! I agree readily. Anything to help him in his work and put our relationship in a better perspective.

Of course, there are those silences between us. At first uncomfortable, they have now become part of the evening. We both have thoughts of our own and no inkling of what the other person is thinking. Then after a lull, we or rather he, remembers that I am there and we pick up the conversation once again.

I love the stillness in the air and the few birds that pass by on their way home. The jasmine tree hangs on the balcony and the scent is both cooling and heady. But most of all, I love the talk we have. I am getting to know my husband a little every day. At first, he was a polite stranger, detached, evincing little interest in what I have to say. I can see he is making an effort though. He asks me if I am happy and before I can answer, he replies himself, "It is too soon to be happy or unhappy. One knows so little about the other. We are both strangers who have taken a gamble with the best possible intentions. A marriage has to be nurtured, to be given time and effort to grow, to prosper, to spread its wings." He tries to be kind while I yearn for affection, he moves my chair when I sit and picks up my tray when it is heavy while all the time I want him to take me in his arms and tell me it will be fine. But our talks continue as talks and we settle into a routine that has no elements of passion, none of fire but rather a force of habit that is not meant for newly weds.

He keeps his distance and my fears of a husband lying on top of me and taking me by force are distant dreams. My vivid imagination, the gruesome horror stories have no reality in my life, for my husband draws back as if burnt when he accidentally touches me.

I wanted to come first with Avinash. Far ahead of everybody else, in a special place of my own that nobody could touch. But things did not work out that way. I might have fooled myself into believing that I had a special place in his affections but very early on life settled down to a humdrum routine where romantic notions and dreams of varying hues found little sustenance and withered away. Avinash was a different person those first few weeks. He had been kind and considerate, even dreamily romantic. He was still kind and considerate but he was becoming distant with each passing day and apart from our wonderful son, we had nothing to hold us together.

In the beginning he would ring from the office, not once, but a number of times. He would try and come home early or even make work at home so he could go late. He would drag Arundhati away form the elaborate shenanigans, the rituals that were part of every household. And no one had said anything. Only now she realised she probably hadn't seen it because it must have been there. She had been blind to the impervious looks of her mother-in-law and numerous aunts; the kind that peered above glasses, the muted and not-so-muted whispers, the frowns of disapproval. Initially she had been blind to it all because she had been insulated form it. She had lived only for Avinash and refused to see beyond him. In the first flush of marriage, it was only natural.

Now everything was different. Avinash came home later and later. He always showered and sat with his mother for what seemed an impossibly long while. By the time he had finished talking to his mother it was time to get ready for some party or the other. Even together, there didn't seem very much to say. Drives to and fro were taken in silence except for a brief word intermittently spoken about something innocuous or the music playing in the background. At parties they went their separate ways and only met on the way back. It was total sham of a marriage.

At first she thought there might be someone else. After all, he had all the ingredients that were attractive to women. He was good looking, immensely wealthy and travelled frequently. The temptation was there, around every corner. But somehow her instinct told her he was not the type to play around. He was much too dignified to stoop to something underhand. But the distance between them, the suspense of not knowing all, took its toll. An inborn dignity had prevented her from spilling her guts all over the carpet. She supposed it had a lot to do with the fact that there was no one who would support her. Her mother-in-law was vehemently pro her son and even if by some remote chance she thought he did or said something wrong, she would never dream of siding with her daughter-in-law. Her sister-in-law was non-commital in every thing. Although an extremely strong person in her own right, she would never oppose her family. There was no one to side with her and she knew anything she said would be futile. So why lose the one thing she had managed to keep intact; her pride and dignity? And that is the way it went. She clung to the shreds of her pride, portraying an outwardly calm façade but there was no doubt in her mind her innards were slowly being eaten away, bit by bit. The accumulated anger, the burning humiliation and raw pain were playing havoc with her mind and emotions.

Before the break, she had reached a turning point in her life. The hours, days and weeks ahead stretched alarmingly into nothingeness. The same old routine and the same old conversations. She was bored stiff of it all. She wanted to be free. She might be in her late thirties and to the world at large, well entrenched in her marriage but that did not mean she was passed it all. She wanted to wear the exciting new designs that were available in clothes instead of the same old sari. Never mind that they were priced in the bracket that most people could not afford. She wouldn't mind going dancing for a change, be taken out for a romantic candle-lit dinner by her husband, even take up some kind of job. She was sick of the same old things, clothes, shopping, the obligatory tete-a-tetes. She wanted more out of her life and she knew she had it in her but how was she going to go about it? She was frightened by the thought that she would never be able to do all that she wanted to and she would continue to live her life like this in meaninglessness.

What a waste, what an absolute waste. Life was too precious to waste, to fritter away in futility. She had to break free of the hypocritical chains that were proving more and more stifling.

There were other things. Avinash was the only man she had ever known. And she had always accepted what was offered. She always thought this was how it must be. But she soon learnt differently. With Tara and Mina, she had been introduced to another world where sex played a major part. They had introduced her to movies and books of a sexual nature that answered her unspoken questions. They also talked openly about lovemaking, different positions and multiple orgasms. Such discussions sent delicious shivers all over her body and awakened her to desires and feelings she had not experienced before.

I am not exactly sure when I found out that not all women found sex repugnant. I think it was a year after we got married. The stories of romance had not prepared me for reality. I knew what the act itself entailed. Today a girl of seventeen is not the innocent she was, say, in my mother's time. Innocent in deed but not in thought. I had, in fact, looked forward to this part of my marriage believing it to be a major contribuant to the bond that existed between a couple. But that, alas, was not the case. Avinash did try, initially. However, I at least never really came to enjoy it. Never in all the years I was married did I find complete fulfilment and so although I knew something was drastically wrong, I never really did anything about it.

At first I had thought that something was wrong with me. It never occurred to me that because no one really wants to talk about their own failure that perhaps there were other women who felt the same way. Or that perhaps there was something wrong with Avinash.

The sex was completely inadequate, unfulfilling and yet disturbing. True, she had nothing to compare it with but still she had seen movies and read books (had she read!) and of course she had heard great stories but never, no never, had that frantic passionate totally mad love making come her way.

Those long, deep soul-searing looks between lovers. The dilating pupils and heavy breathing. The searing urgency and the sound of ripping as clothes were torn apart. The intensity and the passion were always missing. The complete feeling of coming together had never materialised. She could only imagine what it must be like. No, nothing remotely magical had ever happened. It was just lights off, clothes off–if that–and a quick touch here and there on the nipples, a fondle or two for the breast and then penetration. A few pushes and shoves later, Avinash would grunt loudly and it would all be over. He would be snoring in the next few minutes and she would be left ashamed and unsatisfied staring into the darkness.

I know it appears as if Avinash was a completely selfish man, intent on his own satisfaction while completely oblivious to my needs. But I have to be truthful and say that that was not the case at all. Avinash was in fact an extremely caring individual, there was a lot of the softie in him, while what I have just told you paints an entirely variant picture. That of a man who thinks of nothing but his own pleasure. Let me assure you that was not the case at all.

But it bothered her that he had to make such an effort to effect this little display which really satisfied neither.

She was only thirty-six but she felt old. She was always expected to be the dutiful wife with no desires, no dreams or aspirations of her own. She had suppressed them long enough. Now they kept coming back invading her mind, making her conscious of what she was being denied at the oddest of times.

She had been relaxing in the soapy foam of a bubble bath. Maurice Ravel's legendary *Bolero* was playing in the background, a great favourite of hers with its soft beginnings, gradual rising and powerful crescendo. The soothing melody at the start of the piece had insinuated itself into her body's rhythm and together with the warm water from the bath had an increasingly therapeutic effect.

Her body slumped and devoid of any defences was supine. She closed her eyes and let out a deep sigh, thankful for the warm water and the relaxation it afforded her body. She moved her hands a couple of times in the water, splashing it up and down and momentarily disturbing the calm, before the light bubbles and slight tremors of water disappeared again. Eyes still closed, her hands moved to her neck, stroking lightly, them moved to her face, her stomach, stopping for a moment. In the same languid manner, her hands of their own volition went to her vagina. At first she merely stroked her public hair, gently massaging the frothy curls and letting her fingers entwine themselves. For a time, she stopped and let her hand lie on the mound oblivious to everything and just drifting, drifting along.

The music changed. Its beat more insistent, the sound louder and the rhythm faster. Her fingers were no longer lying still. As if in response to some hidden command, they began to move in beat to the music. Then her hand became more insistent; she felt her body slacken as her fingers probed inside, deeper and deeper, slowly and wondrously. Her body's slow and languid movements were replaced now by excited tremors and sudden jerky movements. She felt the excitement building in her, her legs parted wider and wider but then suddenly she stopped. She removed her hand as if she had been burnt.

For a long time after that she had felt guilty and unfulfilled. She knew that if she wanted she could release her frustration but she could not summon up the courage. And the guilt! Oh the guilt! She felt everyone knew. And most definitely her mother-in-law, who in her imagination, kept insinuating all kinds of things.

Everything she said appeared to have an added meaning. It seemed to her that all knew of her indiscretion. She felt more and more ashamed. And yet she couldn't seem to suppress these thoughts and feelings that overcame her. They excited her, removed her from her drab existence and made her feel complete.

How life had changed. Just today, before the party, she had released her pent-up emotions. Her fingers now regularly and of their own accord seemed to find the right spot, the right momentum and before she knew it, she was panting excitedly and squirming like never before. The release when it came was unlike anything she had experienced. The tumultuous feelings, the excitement, the build up and the shuddering release were more than she could bear. The release made her want to cry and scream at the same time. She felt both wanton and immensely fulfilled.

Though she knew this act was not an end in itself, it helped to release some of the emotions that had no other outlet. She recognised it as a stop-gap measure that temporarily lifted her out of her gloom. Initially, there had been moments of guilt when she felt she was committing a crime. But she always countered those feelings with logic. There was nothing bad or unatural about masturbating. It was normal. And deep down she knew this would not be forever.

Often, Arundhati wondered if her husband's shortsightedness was deliberate. After all, they were living in the same house, they shared the same room and though married life had not turned out the way she had envisaged, she was sure he must have some inkling of what she was feeling and what she was going through. But then perhaps he didn't. He was one of those easy-going people who went through life's many vicissitudes with the same staccato comprehension. No leeway was given for the numerous coloured hues and a naturally different understanding of diverse situations. He was not shallow, no never that but nor did his feelings run very deep. And he had never really understood her.

10

She had been born to obey. Right from the day she could remember she had always been doing someone else's bidding. If it was not her father or her mother then it was her darling brother. Not that she minded. She doted on all of the them and her brother had a special place in her affection from the moment he was born. But she hated the loveless obligations foisted on her from the moment she got married.

Life had becomel a meaningless routine. She went through the obligatory charade of touching her mother-in-law's feet to denote respect, kept her head covered, not fully, but enough in her presence and yet at the end of all these years, she could not say that each side knew the other at all. Time had passed in senseless rituals but real companionship and affection had never been forged. She was nothing more than a mechanical robot in her presence. In her mother-in-law's presence, her speech was stilted, her answers automatic. Her mother-in-law did not care to see why her daughter-in-law did not laugh or indeed if she ever did, what her dreams were or her feelings on any issue. She was, after all, the daughter-in-law of Mrs Anirudh Diwan, no small matter that, and had to mould herself to the prevalent system her mother-in-law had and hers before her. Sympathy of any kind was out of the question as was breaking with the prevalent system.

She touched her in-laws' feet every morning, did the *puja* and saw to the breakfast. After seeing her husband and son off, she took a shower and then went to sit with her mother-in-law. That was obligatory. There was no question of skipping one day or doing it at a later time. She had to adhere to a set pattern just as her mother-in-law had and her mother-in-law before her. By that time half the morning was almost over and she had a little time to herself before it was lunch and her son came back.

In the afternoons she would rest or sit with her son and then around 4.30 she would have tea with her mother-in-law. By the time she finished this tradition bound ritual she would do the *puja* and prepare for her husband's homecoming. Once he arrived, they were off to some social event or party of his. She went to bed after all the others and lay awake wondering if this was what life had in store for her or was there something more? She knew they had to be but when she questioned her mother or tentatively broached her husband, she was rebuffed from both quarters.

I would touch my mother-in-law's feet every morning. In return, I would receive a few formal words that were as distant and as glacial as the freezing temperatures in the early hours of the hilly mornings. Initially, there would be an awkward pause, while I would just stand around not knowing what to do. Should I stand or sit, talk or keep quiet? At first, I would be out of her room faster than a juggler at his job but it would make matters worse when I saw disapproval writ large on her face.

Despite the many years of living together, I had never managed to break through her reserve. I received the same curt monosyllabic replies to my queries. She never seemed to realise the effort it required to ask those predetermined questions and thought she was selfish and singularly lacking in gratitude, after all I could just as easily have left her alone!

"Good morning, *mama ji,*" I would say enthusiastically, summoning the biggest possible smile to my face.

"Good morning," she would reply in a distant whisper. So faint it was almost impossible to catch the faint strains and often I would turn away believing she had not responded to my greeting. It was a ruse of hers. She loved to see my discomfort and of course there was nothing like causing real despair.

"What are you plans today? Are you going out or will you be staying at home?" I would chirrup loudly, marvelling at my acting prowess.

"I don't know yet," she wold reply more often than not and would move away leaving me feeling like a complete fool.

Over the years, we developed a mutual disregard for each other that was enveloped in tones of formality. I think we both shrank from a public display of our apathy. I often wonder why I never chose to live away from her. The joint family system was undergoing great strains and several well-established families were going the new way. I was amazed to find mother and daughters-in-law who did nothing but bicker when they lived under one roof, after living separately were now regularly seen lunching together and going out on shopping trips as if they had always been the best of friends. Apart from a distaste of washing my private laundry in public and adding fodder to a society that thrived on gossip, I genuinely thought it wrong to leave my mother-in-law on her own. If her husband had been alive, well it might have been different, but I doubt it. I think secretly I couldn't face the fact that I had failed. Not being on good terms with my mother-in-law was a failure.

She remembered as a young bride when she had entered the house and hoped for love and affection from her mother-in-law but the disdain with which she had been treated had led her to keep her distance forever.

Arundhati often wondered where she had gone wrong.

Initially, she had believed she could win over anyone and surmount any difficulty. She had been young enough to mould herself to what was expected of her from her husband and his family but still, her mother-in-law refused to bend her will and truly accept her.

Arundhati chuckled to herself. The one thing her mother-in-law had not bargained for was her indefatigible will and spirit that could not countenance what was wrong or prejudiced. But ultimately she had suffered for she had only alienated herself further while her mother-in-law moved on implacably.

The party had gained in momentum, much to the satisfaction of the hosts. Soon food was being served and the guests who had not managed to lose themselves to some intoxicating aphrodisiac moved with enthusiasm towards the tables. Each table was covered with the finest cotton table-cloths specially imported from Egypt. They were covered with intricate floral patterns painstakingly sewn by several hands working to create a piece of art.

The crockery and cutlery were both sterling silver, right from the huge soup tureens, the *thaalis* and serving spoons to the smallest teaspoon, the little chutney holders and the napkin holders. The silver display spoke volumes of the lavishness and immense wealth of the hosts. In an age of fast food and convenience, silver utensils were a dying breed. True, the obligatory silver was still used, but this was a spectacular display. Nowadays, who had the time to polish such a vast array of utensils like they did in the old days?

Apart from the silver the many tables were fairly groaning under the profusion of dishes laid out in splendour. Authentic *tandoori peshawari* cuisine; *naan, malai* chicken and creamy butter *dal* from the North-West Frontier beckoned invitingly. Exotic Thai and Chinese spring-rolls, *dim sums* and *tom yum* soup intermingled on another table while yet the third, allured with continental bakes, Italian *pasta*, Swiss *rosti* and Greek *mezzes*.

There was a beautiful flower arrangement at the centre of each table; a vast array of gladioli, lillies, tube-roses and marigolds.

11

It was the small things in life, the day-to-day happenings, thought Arundhati, that left an impression on you. She remembered when she was newly married, she had hated eating vegetables like *tori, arbi* and *kadu* and had made her dislike apparent. It was something which she was never allowed to forget. Her mother-in-law was forever making oblique remarks and snide references. After all, her daughter had adjusted so well. A fussy eater before her marriage, she now ate everything without a murmur. Arundhati found this attitude highly hypocritical.

Did that mean that only in your parents' house could you be yourself, your true self but once you went to your in-laws you had to always hide behind a veil of superficiality? If you didn't like something, you still went along with it. For what? To please them. But what pretence. So unnecessary and so superficial.

The *bahu* thought of her in-laws' house as a place where a façade was needed to make them think better of her. She did not realise that it did not matter to them at all. And her parents' house was her home where she could let her hair down and become her true self. Here she could expect indulgence and love. Why could it not happen there? By her pretence, she was making life difficult for herself. Arundhati felt it was always better to be upfront and be what you were than try to hide behind subterfuge.

But there was subterfuge everywhere. She knew a lot of her so-called friends were really fair-weather friends. They were friends because of her name, who she was and the people she knew. They were attracted to her car outside, the fancy address and the fact that she travelled abroad so often. Apart from that they did not care. What her thoughts were, her feelings, her desires; these were of little or no consequence. After all, what did it have to do with them?

She felt a gnawing discontent that started at dawn and spent the whole day with her. Sometimes it would keep her awake for hours and she would lie in bed tossing from side to side feeling unfulfilled and often unsatisfied. She began to question everything.

She was doing nothing with her life. What was she... .nothing more than an ornamental piece like the *Morano* fish in the drawing room or the *Lalique* toucan that Avinash had lovingly displayed in the study. And even that was treated with more reverence!

She had had enough of it all. The kitty parties that stretched into endless boring hours where everyone tried to outdo the other from what was worn to the food that was cooked. It was really quite pathetic when you thought about it. Women who had nothing of substance in their lives and were extremely vacuous not to mention downright boring. And what were the hot topics of conversation? Well....the best was if someone had bought some new piece of jewellery, then that topic occupied the entire lunch or if someone was going abroad – Europe, Australia, the far East– these were the current hot spots. There would be sighs of envy and again each vied with the other on giving advice to show they had been there the last year or the one before...all in a bid not to be outdone!

At an idle moment in the party, I espied Mrs Singh doing her utmost to be the gracious hostess. When she moved towards me, I could not help wondering what she must look like without her corset. The thought was so hilarious, I could not help laughing aloud and it was a few minutes before I heard what she was saying.

"Arundhati!" a friend of hers nudged me reprovingly. I glanced at her cursorily. She was one of Mrs Singh's fans, the many that dotted the landscape. Vacuous painted faces with nothing to their credit except their well-to-do husbands who allowed them the freedom to shop till they dropped. And thus, command some kind of peripheral place in society.

"I'm so sorry, Mrs Singh," I said. "What did you say?"

She did not like that, not being heard and having to repeat herself.

"I was saying," she said with a faint smile, "that I recently commissioned Sandip Rai to do an exclusive painting for me. It just came in this evening and there was no time to put it up."

"Would you like to see it?"

There was nothing I could do but feign enthusiasm and satisfied, she led us on.

I did not care much for this particular artist but the painting was one of the worst examples of his work I had ever seen and it looked like he had fobbed it off on her rather than doing a special piece. But before I could even say anything neutral, there were gasps and sighs of admiration all around. More guests were crowding around Mrs Singh asking her all kinds of questions and I could see her bask in the glory of it all. Never mind that, most of the guests didn't know a thing about art but were prey to gallery-owners that had sprouted like mushrooms everywhere and had become the new connossieurs. All that was of no consequence. What was important was they had been told the artist was a great buy and they had followed blindly. Liking it didn't actually come into it all.

Arundhati moved quietly away from the group and went out to the balcony.

She saw Jai Kumar, the journalist, putting a *paan* in his mouth, his mind and whole body engaged in this task. She thought of her local *paan-wallah* whom she saw two or three times a week. The man was used to seeing her and they would chat amicably, in fact, he had become something of a friend, if such friendships existed. He was an old man whose son had helped him set up the shop after he had retired from his job as a train driver. His failing eyesight had ended his job and instead of sitting at home doing nothing, he had decided to take on this job. It kept him busy and it prevented him from feeling useless.

"Well, *kaka* how are you today?" she asked smilingly.

"*Namaste beti*, everything is going well, thanks to God." And without asking, he started making her *paans*. He knew she would take four sweet with extra *gulgandh*.

While she waited, she asked him about his family. His daughter had got married a month ago and already the demands were coming in. He had discussed the groom with her before the marriage. It seemed they wanted too much money and she had told him so but eventually he had bowed under pressure and given them the black and white television and the pressure cooker. Never mind that barely two months ago he had given them a transistor radio, a now defunct *Hitkari* tea-set which he had managed to buy second hand. One of the cups had a slight mark on it which was what enabled him to buy it in the first place but his daughters-in-law had discovered the mark and sent the set back. He was scared of what they would do to his daughter which was why he was giving in to their demands.

She felt very humbled when she listened to him. This was reality. This was life. She lived in a world where the troubles that plagued her kind were as remote as the snow-capped mountains in Switzerland. She felt all the more the gloss and superficiality of the life she was living. Her problems were the extra pimple on her face, what dress to wear and the fact that the servant was an hour late coming in.

12

Although we were not close, I slowly grew to understand this man I had married. He was not atypical, a particular type of married man. He hardly spent time at home and would often exhibit a restlessness when proximity loomed large. You could see he was feeling constricted. He was a decidedly different person with his son and it was because he saw him as a friend, with no demands imposed upon him. He was hardly your average family man.

Her husband was essentially a good man. She realisd that part of the problem was she was an absolute romantic. Everything was viewed through the haze of the ultimate; the *grand passion.* And anything less was just not good enough. So she was always looking for the grand finale to end things, the grand gesture, the swooning and the passion. But marriage to Avinash had not encapsulated her dreams into reality and nothing can ever compete with the perception one has in the imagination. The interpretation of feelings. High drama and tension were all part of what she expected from her relationship, what she yearned for. It was like a play in which she was the star and her husband, who could not comprehend or even dream of what she was thinking, was as best an outsider. It was frustrating for both of them. He realised very early on the terrible mistake he had made. She was no level-headed, down-to-earth woman who would settle down to domestic harmony devoid of imagination and lacking in affection. This was a woman of great passion, of great depth. She expected more than most from life because she believed it was essential to her, as essential as her breathing. She was also willing to give of her self completely. He understood part of her, the other part was a mystery. It forever eluded him and it was a pressure keeping up with her. At times he almost gave up.

Nobody guessed they had a problem. On the face of it they were an extremely affectionate couple. There was no excessive cooing and petting in public. But still, looking at them, one would not have realised anything was wrong.

She felt guilty all the time. But though she tried to suppress her thoughts, they kept coming back. The fact was she had lasted this long because she kept thinking what a genial person Avinash was and how good he was to her. She thought about her family, how horrified they would be. Her mother-in-law would use the oppurtunity to bare her fangs. And, most importantly, Rajeev, her son, her darling son, what disastrous effect would it have on him?

She felt on edge constantly. Stretching, straining at every nerve. She felt she was living on the edge of a precipice and any moment she would tumble over. She was on a short fuse and got upset on the slightest provocation. She knew she could not last long like this.

It was a funny situation to be in. Sometimes, she felt like an observer viewing her own feelings. She loved Avinash and had grown to love him because he was an innately good person, because he was the father of her child, because he tried to be kind and considerate. Because. . . because . . .there were so many reasons. But though she loved him, he did not possess her heart. And she knew it was not enough. She felt compassion for both of them. In moments of intuition she knew they were *both* suffering.

She could not penetrate his mind, he plainly did not

understand her feelings, her expressions, the words were all wrong. Each discourse left both feeling more upset and more vulnerable.

Indeed, when I look back upon those distressing days, the emotion I remember the best is anger. Anger at being forced into a situation I did not want and my helplessness against it. But later on it changed to a dull smouldering resentment against my husband and my in-laws. It was a feeling that was always present with me. It was a feeling that somewhere and somehow I had been cheated. Most times, I did not let these feelings surface but who can really guard against the subconscious? When I least expected to I would erupt over the smallest of issues and the feeling of discontent would be overwhelming.

I would often ask myself if I was one of those sad creatures who went through life seeking something and somehow never finding it. Simply because they didn't know what they were looking for. It was heartbreaking. All my life I thought I had almost found what I was searching for but it had always eluded me. Marriage had satiated me for a time. The humdrum events of everyday life had kept me busy but now my feelings of despair threatened to overwhelm me. I was slowly suffocating and I did not know what to do about it.

She knew many women went through life grateful for the little they got. Why she cursed herself did she have to be so greedy? But another voice inside her berated her for feeling so helpless and weak. If only she saw beyond the narrowness of herself and those around her.

Could she live alone? Women today were doing it all the time. The stigma was still there but what the hell, it was her life. No one else was going to help her. She was too much of a dreamer, she lived on the sidelines of life while actuality was all in her head and so far she had managed to get through on that. There were no easy solutions. She was trapped for now. Why did human beings always have to hanker for something? Those truly contented people were a rarity.

The case of Nafisa, a friend of hers, came to mind. She left her husband and child, and walked out after four years of marriage, leaving behind a certain security and for what is was worth a marriage in name, that provided her with the accoutrements required for living. She must have been really desperate to do so. To give up a secure existence for the unknown with no means of support. But what made her sick were comments like "She must be having an affair, otherwise why would she leave?" or "even if she could not adjust she should have continued living her life even if it was one of misery."

So wrongs were to be endured and perpetuated because other people had suffered them, and had been unable to stand up to society, perhaps becoming bitter in the process. That bitterness and cowardice were making other people suffer. How narrow and contemptuous people were. Most people were essentially cowards. They derived their strength from numbers.

How was one to live in such a society? One where hypocrisy and contempt played a large part. Rules were adhered to but when they suited you. Backbiting and bitching were life and from day-to-day your friends changed depending on your own social and economic position. And she wanted none of it. She knew she had to stay away, for to stay was to be sucked into the system, which like it or not, enslaved you before you had any real chance to think of any other alternative.

Time wore heavily on Arundhati and when you are unhappy it seems to bear down more oppressively. She had never been the kind of person who is at ease in kitty gatherings, social parties and the showy charity committees that proclaimed their largesse before the deed was even completed. People thought she was snobbish when she was essentially reserved. The fact that she was rich didn't help. It was said she thought no end of herself because of her money.

In some ways she had given up. Otherwise, why the endless social parties with its constant chitter-chatter that was essential. She had allowed herself to be part of a society that was basically ruthless and only bothered with you if you were "up to the mark" and Arundhati was certainly someone of consequence. But Arundhati did not place herself in that category. She had never cared whether someone belonged to a wealthy family or were themselves somebody. If she liked you, she liked you for who you were.

Along with the "right friend" went the "right kind of place." There was a definite need to be seen in all the right places. It could be the opening of a new boutique by a hot-shot designer, the latest art exhibition that one just had to see, the launch of a new spa, a reading session by an up coming writer, more for the purpose of saying one met him or her which in later versions would change to knowing the author intimately! For most social climbers, it was important to have those few minutes of actuality which would act as a central point from which the imaginative yarns could be based on.

It was a cruel society that fed off the misfortunes of others. Everyone was in a hurry to reach the top and anything or anyone that came in the way was pushed aside. If you happened to fall, well, that was your own problem. Wealth was of paramount importance. It was the new god. Family connections also counted. But it was the wheeling and dealing, the people you knew, the places you were seen at that largely determined what others thought of you. Thus, the old cousins who had never risen were conveniently forgotten. The eponymous Sharma *sahib* useful in his time as a top bureaucrat had since retired and over the years his usefulness had diminished. Of course, sometimes when it was essential and his influence still counted for something, he was called and had to do what was necessary, a phone here, a word there, but then he was relegated to the background once again.

Take the party today. It was being given by a couple whose fortunes dipped precariously from time to time but they managed to surface with amazing alacrity. He was an executive with a foreign multinational, she an interior decorator of sorts. They had immediately got into the social scene with gusto giving parties which were exclusive and thereby talked about. And naturally with the kind of clout he wielded and the vast sums of money he threw around as well as his wife's burgeoning business, they were invited everywhere. But when the company had decided to withdraw from the country, he lost his job and with it the requisite perks; the imported car, the bevy of servants, the beautiful house and the entertainment allowance. They were no longer considered part of the *must* category and very quickly they were dropped from people's lists. His wife enjoyed her own clientele but as a consequence of her husband's fall from grace, she no longer had the most exclusive clients. She now catered to anyone with money and since the discernment had disappeared it soon became a fall of double consequence.

But he had not gone underground and disappeared. No. He had joined another foreign company and got himself an even better deal. And so they were back in the party circuit again. In society, one had to be thick-skinned. Neither husband or wife gave any indication of the trauma they underwent or how upset they were when everyone turned their backs on them. They understood the game. It was all a matter of who you were and what you had to offer. Friendship, loyalty and matters dealing with emotion had no place here. Money, wealth, connections; that was what counted.

Arundhati watched an old Lady surreptitiously pocket some food from the over-laden dinner table. She was her mother's friend and was notorious for taking home leftover scraps from parties or even weddings. People called it "the eccentricity of the rich." The plain truth was the woman desperately needed to be hospitalised. But then the rich lived by rules of their own.

13

Arundhati saw her brother chatting with a group of friends. He was enjoying himself and why shouldn't he, she asked herself. Not everyone had made a mess of their lives.

I wish I could recapture the early years of love and innocence. I remember the first few years of my childhood passing in spoilt contentment. Suddenly after eight glorious years a brother appeared and I had to share him with Amah. I watch in curiosity as he grows every day and moves from crawling to walking.

As a child, I was ugly. I was too tall and too thin. My hair was braided constantly and smelt of Amah's coconut oil. My features were nondescript except for my teeth which gave me a look not unlike bugs bunny and would later have to be corrected with the help of braces. My brother, on the other hand, was a good looking baby. He was fair to my dark, with curly hair and the deepest of dimples. He was also winsome and cuddly and I was constantly hearing the words *choo chweet* from his adoring female following. He also had big liimpid eyes with the longest eyelashes. I once tried pulling them off hoping to stick them on to mine which were much shorter. But he screamed so loudly, I lost my nerve and had to constantly bribe him not to tell Amah.

Amah is just as proud of him as I am if not more and loves taking him for a stroll in his pram. Inevitably, some passerby stops to look at him and comment on his good looks. She loves it when they ask if he has any foreign blood for she believes he is a real *sahib* and it elevates her status in the eyes of the other *ayahs*.

I should by right have hated him especially when Amah

changed her allegiance but I did not. I adored him and was in fact his chief fan. But that is my secret. I never let on how much I loved him. So I constantly baited him and aggravated him to get his undivided attention. Very early on, I found it worked wonders instead of being mushy and sentimental.

He is named Anirudh but I call him *Nikka*, which means "younger brother." For a long time, he responds to this name but later on he changes it to Nick. He was planning to go to America for further studies and decided Nick would be easy to pronounce and there was no need to go into explanations because of the extra *a*.

We sleep together at night with Amah on a mat by our side. I loved those times and remember them with fond memories. In winter, the warmth and cosiness of the quilt as we snuggled together to rid ourselves of the cold. The bed was warm with hot-water bottles and we would squeal in pleasure as our cold bodies touched the heated surface. When I thought he was fast asleep, I would snuggle closer to him and plant wet kisses all over his face and sometimes squeeze him tight. If he was fast asleep, nothing would happen but sometimes he was only half asleep and would squeal angrily and turn away from me.

The summer months were tortuous and we felt hot and languid. I was secretly terrified he would want to sleep separately but he never said anything except complain as we all did about the overwhelming heat.

We had our own rooms by the time I was teenager. I needed my own space I told my mother rather pompously not realising how much I was going to miss those giggling nights filled with silly imaginings and innocent fights. The next five years passed in a whirl of teenage activity and we were both preoccupied with our own separate worlds. I was married at seventeen and everything changed after that.

Just before I got married, he put a toad in my bed. I

hadn't understood the earlier giggling, the desire to be with me in my room or the false cajoling to sleep early. Ordinarily, I would have recognised the signs but I was overwrought and anxious about my impending marriage and overlooked the mischievous looks and hushed laughter. I got into bed and switched off the lights. It was a few minutes before I heard the croak in my ear and knew there was something other than me in my bed. I screamed and screamed while my brother hurried into my room bursting with laughter. "Before you find your prince, you have to kiss a frog," he chirped happily jumping up and down. He was, of course, severely reprimanded and Amah was allowed to sleep close to me that night.

I remembered the incident when soon after Avinash left me I found, this time thankfully the cute and cuddly variety, in my bed. I knew what my brother was saying and I hoped one day my prince would appear.

14

Avinash watched Arundhati on the swing. He thought about going up to her but hesitated when he saw the glazed look on her face. It was not unlike the expression he had seen when he first met her.

Her beautiful face had a set expression and I could see that she was in some kind of shock. At first I thought it might be the difficult situation that had made her feel this way or even the realisation that the moment of meeting had arrived. I felt ill-at-ease and wished I could regain my normal confidence for if I was feeling this way, the poor child must be going through a gruelling time.

As Avinash had correctly surmised she was in shock, but it was the shock of realising that all her pent-up dreams and fantasies had not materialised.

I was charmed by what I saw. An extremely beautiful and intelligent child. For that is what she was at that moment – a child. I saw the great promise for the future, she would one day turn into a beautiful woman. One with great strength and sensitivity.

I used her for my own purpose. Why shouldn't I? I was twenty-eight having just returned from abroad, the talisman of the successful. I had finished my studies and was all set to join the family business of oil, construction, textiles and leather products after having been given enough time to sow my wild oats if the corny old term was still used today. I had long since found out where my sexual preference lay and had followed my true nature abroad. But here back in the country where a man's name meant everything and one was recognised immediately I got cold feet. All my well-thought-out plans, of convincing my mother, vanished the moment I saw her at the house. As the car drew up inside the wide driveway, I saw my mother standing straight and aloof, her head covered not in subjugation but part of a long tradition. I lost my nerve and submitted to the ordeal fate had chosen for me.

Of course, my mother loved me but it was a remote and distant love. I do not remember her ever hugging or kissing me. Physical demonstrativeness had never been encouraged and as a child I soon learnt not to show my affection openly, especially towards my mother.

Well at any rate, I realised then at that moment that I was going to have to rethink my entire ideas. I just did not have the guts to tell her. And when she along with my father and numerous relatives suggested marriage, I went along meekly like the proverbial lamb to the slaughter.

If I had another brother may be that would have helped but since I was the only son there was no way I could shirk my responsibilities. And my sister was of no help. She had since married and embraced her new household with all the passion and virtuosity of the recently initiated.

When I saw Arundhati so soft and shy, so much the little lady I knew, I had nothing to fear. I could marry and even be happy with a gentle creature like her. If I thought about her at all, her feelings and what she was to get out of this marriage, they were soon quashed. I admit I was selfish, more than that I was needlessly cruel and an utter coward. I ruined her life because I couldn't face my own. In fact, initially I did try. Really. And it seemed to work. She was such a young girl. Barely having turned seventeen. I moulded her the way I wanted. She had breeding and a definite manner. She was beautiful and although I could appreciate it as one might an exquisite piece of art, physically it left me cold. Sleeping with her was not the easiest of tasks but since she did not know any better, I think I performed well and she didn't seem to want for anything else.

How little I really knew and how foolish to think one can deceive oneself by masking one's inner feelings.

She was taller than I had imagined for I had heard she was a very tall girl. Her figure was exquisite. I could see the immaculate curves through the sheer chiffon *salwar kameez.* She had beautiful skin, smooth and creamy, high cheekbones, soft hazel eyes with long eyelashes and a slender long neck. I was hoping to find her unattractive, so I could give a valid reason for refusing to marry her but I knew there was no way I could refuse her now. She was stunning. I almost lost my composure as I realised there was no way out but with a great amount of effort, I managed to maintain a neutral expression and started asking the right kind of questions.

We spent a few evenings together and I realised what an innocent she was. On evening, it was later than usual and I dropped her to her room. A momentary impulse overtook me and I kissed her on her cheek as one would a good friend or even a younger niece. It was innocent and light-hearted. Just as I was withdrawing from her, she turned her head and probably with the same impulsiveness that had seized me a moment ago grazed my mouth with her own.

I knew it was not a premeditated act nor did it have the touch of an experienced woman but it had a lingering sensuousness that should have alerted my senses, awakened me to the danger and the grave act I was going to commit by marrying her. At that moment, I was too startled to do anything than brush it off and she, mortified by her forwardness, withdrew to the comfort of her room.

I don't know what I was thinking, the only excuse was that I wasn't thinking at all. I didn't know how I was going to keep a woman happy when what I really wanted was to be in the arms of another man. Maybe I thought she was one of those upper crust women who looked upon sex as a necessary act of conceiving rather than a pleasure in itself. But I knew subconsciously from that previous moment that Arundhati wasn't a woman of emotions. Her feeling ran deep and for her sex was a further bond between two couples who had promised to share their lives together. How could I have wrecked her life so knowingly just to protect mine? And I should have really known that marriage in itself would be no protection but the destruction of more lives.

For the first few years of our marriage we seemed happy. I was temporarily content and she was a good wife. She never asked for the things I had in abundance and would have willingly showered on her. But what she did ask for was more and more affection and I knew the few times when I rebuffed her she felt it deeply. Eventually our son was born and she seemed to transfer her affection from me to him. I cannot say I was not relieved because I was but a part of me was deeply saddened by the hurt I had caused and which no matter what I did, I could never undo.

And as she spent more time with the boy, I felt the noose loosen slightly and I let myself drift into the inevitable. I spent more time away from home. More business trips, more late nights – the usual pattern. The web was intricately spun.

Every time, Arundhati commented on my absence, I would irritatedly push it aside because I was scared and frustrated without realising that all the while the volcano was slowly . . .ever so slowly, spewing its lava.

It set a kind of pattern and eventually she stopped asking me questions. In a way, I was grateful the questions had stopped and eventually the guilt which was driving me crazy was replaced by a stupid and selfish logic that is invariably resorted to when one has succumbed fully and seeks only to satisfy his inner voice. After all said the voice: "She was well married to one of the best families in the country. She had all the creature comforts she could ask for. She had a beautiful son and he was a perfect husband in public. He was attentive and caring in front of others. Not that he was demonstrative, but kind and considerate."

She stopped asking him why he was coming home later and he stopped having think up vague excuses. She gradually understood that it couldn't just be work and realised there must be another woman or other women but she left it at that. She never really probed or questioned anything too deeply. She had built a wall around herself which kept her well insulated and she had no desire to give herself more heartbreak.

I appear weak, a coward, utterly spineless and I was. I thought it better to hide behind a veil of respectability than tear down the false norms which rule one's life. I realise that we are all slaves to society and its conventions so why put further pressure on oneself by adding more rules. I am a happier man now that my secret is out in the open. I feel blessed to have a son such as Rajeev. My only regret is what I have done to Arundhati. She gave of herself so trustingly and I callously destroyed that trust. The guilt will remain with me forever. The only consolation I have is that she has chosen to be my friend, to forgive me rather than let me burn in the fire. She is an amazing woman and I pray she finds a better man than I am.

Arundhati surveyed the party scene and her moving eyes soon alighted on Avinash. He was deep in thought. She could tell he was reliving the past. She sensed his pain just as she had sensed his inner yearning while refusing to recognise it.

Something was going on. Avinash had been behaving very oddly of late. I couldn't put my finger on anything concrete. One incident, however, made an impression.

We were watching a movie late at night on the television. It was a love story in two parts and the suspense had me waiting eagerly all day to see what the villain was going to do now that he had found the girl of his dreams in a passionate embrace with his enemy. I loved these mushy serials where love triumphed over evil. They didn't usually have very explicit love scenes but this serial was an exception. I had already watched some rather heavy petting and now here was an extremely graphic sex scene. I admit I liked watching these scenes especially if the scene was between two lovers as was happening now.

It was not too long ago that such scenes were not shown on television. Just as couples were going to kiss and we would see their lips inching forward; slowly, ever so slowly. . .woosh! the scene would abruptly disappear and we would hear sudden music in the background followed by the picture of a flower. For what seemed an interminable time, we would be privy to the different positions from which one can view a flower. It was rather idiotic and one got fed up of seeing so many flowers! These sudden changes were extremely ridiculous and did not serve the purpose they were intended for. Instead of erasing the image from one's mind they embedded it further by attempting to eliminate thus making its obviousness all the more obvious. It disrupted the flow one was in and invarably put me in a bad mood.

Avinash hated these scenes and would for some odd reason want to talk to me at that very moment. I always found this foible of his strange and vaguely disturbing.

"Arundhati, can you get me some water?" or "did you read the papers today?" "I wanted to talk to you about the party we are planning next week. . . ." The list of things he needed to say right at that particular moment were infinite. I found it extremely irritating that he wanted to discuss these particular points right then between those graphic scenes.

Well, to get back to this particular incident. After a while, we found the villain enjoying the advances of another man. I thought he would push the man away and display some of the evil temper we had been witness to earlier but rather surprisingly he did not and instead succumbed to the man. This was an unexpected twist and I turned to ask Avinash if he was as surprised as I was.

He was sitting upright and his face was only partially revealed in the darkness but there was enough light from the television screen to show the emotions on his face. Apart from watching with rapt attention something I was personally uncomfortable with, he had a look of such intense joy. I gasped involuntarily and then put my knuckles in my mouth to stop myself from saying anything.

He did not seem to be aware of me. His eyes were transfixed on the screen, his hands which moments ago had been tapping impatiently on his knee were curled and taut and he appeared to be enjoying the scene intensely. No, that is not quite right. "Enjoying" does not quite describe what I mean. "Identifying" would be more appropriate. Yes, that's it. He was actively identifying with the scene as if it was something he was familiar with. His breathing was ragged and I could see his chest heaving rapidly. At one point he called out involuntarily, turned towards me with a glazed look on his face and with beads of perspiration forming on his forehead and upper lip. He no longer seemed to be aware of his surroundings and I could feel him gradually mesh with what was happening in front of us.

His body began to twitch spamodically and his breathing got heavier. His pupils were slightly dilated and all the while I just stared wondering how all this had come about. I touched his hand tentatively. It was hot and sticky. Avinash was in the habit of moving his toes, twitching them every few seconds as if to reassure himself they were there. Now, however, they were completely still, absolutely rigid which was very unlike the usual Avinash.

I turned towards the screen. The lovemaking on the television was extremely graphic along with a variety of noises and heavy breathing. Although I had no personal distaste for lesbian and gay relationships, believing each person chose the way he or she wanted to live, such liaisons were still not understood in our country. Nevertheless, I could not help feeling slightly sick when I looked at the screen. Sick because it showed up my husband in a light I had hitherto not seen or chosen not to see.

When the villain and the older man reached a shuddering climax and the scene moved to another one of dialogue, Avinash lay back on the pillows and heaved a deep sigh as if he had actually been part of that scene. He looked at me with a contented smile on his face and then quickly replaced it with a blank look when he saw my partially questioning and partly incredulous look.

There was an awkward silence for a long moment. Both of us looked away from each other. I didn't know what to say. There were too many thoughts exploding in my mind simultaneously. Then Avinash rose saying the movie was boring and he was going to have a shower. I didn't respond but I was perturbed by those naked emotions I had witnessed on his face.

I did not mention the incident again. I think I deliberately blotted it out of my mind, though it hovered in the background threatening to break out at the slightest provocation. Days went by according to its set pattern but there was an overhanging cloud. Something ...someone...had to break the impasse, the impending feeling of doom.

It was Avinash who came looking for me and said, "we have to talk to each other." I sensed the moment of truth. I was in a trance where my normally agile mind was completely numb and I seemed to have lost my power of speech.

We were in our bedroom. A beautiful creation of silks and satins that I had spent many hours deliberating upon. The drapes were light blue with a creamy flower motive running through it, the counterpane was a matching colour though printed and the furniture was light period. The room was large enough to accommodate a four-poster bed which I had entwined in white muslin on all four corners. The pristine white marble floor was covered with silk carpets in pastel colours that further heightened the delicacy of the room. There were many flowers in crystal vases and delicate cut-glass pieces. I had put a lot of effort into decorating this room and I was pleased with its soft feminine ambience.

From a great distance I heard Avinash tell me he was a homosexual. I heard him say how sorry he was and the last thing he wanted to do was to hurt me. "It's the way I am Arundhati, it's just the way I am."

I wanted to cry, to scream, to lash out at him in all my pent-up rage and frustration.

He looked at me raging inwards, he knew that look on my face. "I am truly sorry I have hurt you, it wasn't my intention, I tried to conceal this from you, even deny myself in the beginning but I can't . . . I just can't."

I knew the agony, the great frustration and torture, the indecisiveness that must have been behind this final decision to bare his soul. But at that moment it all seemed very easy, the words falling from his lips as if he were uttering some commonplace. And it made me angry.

"You just can't?" I shouted in anger. "You just can't? Well, what about me, what am I going to do with the rest of my life? I've been a complete and utter fool. If you knew how you felt why in God's name did you marry me? Why did you have to ruin my life?"

I could feel myself trembling, my iron-cast self-control seemed to be slipping away and I felt like killing him. I rushed forward and began hitting him, anywhere I could, all the while saying the most dreadful and cruel things. I called him all kinds of names but he did not react. Not a word as he took my abuse and the beating passively.

Finally, totally spent, we stared at each other in silence. There was nothing more to be said. The truth was there before me unencumbered having broken free of its shackles and could no longer be denied. My husband was a homosexual who had finally freed himself from what must obviously have been years of torture and stepped out to claim another partner, another life. He was refusing to live a lie any longer; "I no longer want to live with lies and subterfuge. Nothing can change what I am and so I refuse to live in pretence any longer."

I was humiliated but more than that I was saddened by the obvious loss and the inevitable change in our lives. I had married this man very young and for a long time he had been my whole world, now I felt lost and alone. I wanted to try and understand him but I felt nothing, nothing but an overwhelming sense of failure.

I was being cast aside for another man. I couldn't quite comprehend it. I suppose I could fight a woman, after all we were the same and one understood what one was up against, but a man, a *man*, how could I ever compete with that. I was being rejected for being a woman and there was no way Avinash was going to go back to what he was not.

"What," I stammered, "will we tell Rajeev?"

He pulled a chair close to mine and looked at me directly. "I'm tired of the pretence, of the lying and all the subterfuge that goes with it. I want to live life as a free spirit not someone constantly hampered by lies and deceit."

I did not know what to say or what to think and kept asking, "But what about Rajeev?"

"Well what about him?" he said.

"What will he say when he finds out, how do you think he will feel?"

"He will have to know sooner or later. I refuse, absolutely refuse to go through the kind of hell I have been living in any longer. My values, my ideas about life, have always been different from yours. I am different from you and I would rather my child knew me for what I am and respect me for being honest with him than to find out later and despise me for it."

I was seething with anger and in those moments I hated him more than I have ever hated anyone.

I will myself to sleep but it is of no use. I stare into the blank ceiling reliving the whole nightmare and saying all the things I should and could have said but was too stricken at that time to do more than comprehend what Avinash was saying. I devised numerous schemes, different scenarios all ending with Avinash's humiliation. I had been *hurt*, a tame word to describe the fire that burnt like hot coals within me and was threatening to engulf me unless I found an outlet which would act like cool water and let out the steam.

Time stands still as I put together the fragments, those infinitely minute pieces that sum up my life. In one scenario, I forgo my pride and behave the way I was brought up to, with loathing and disdain. In this scene, Avinash being nothing more than a lowly human being is allowed his craving, while the woman he made his vows to, namely me, lives in impeccable solitude. In another, I forget everything and live life on a precarious balance deliberately blotting out the past and with nothing to look forward to in the future.

None of the scenes are to my liking and I have to eventually stop day-dreaming. There is no other way. I must accept Avinash and the choice he has made realising that it will do me no good to hold on to something that has never truly belonged to me.

With understanding comes some measure of peace and I prefer it this way. I must let go of my widow's mourning for I am neither. It is better to have him as a friend and give in to the luxury of finding myself as a woman, something that neither of us ever grasped, than to lose everything and perhaps myself in the process.

I never asked who he was spending his time with. As strange as it may seem, I really did not want to find out. I know it sounds defeatist as if I had given up on life but that is only when you make the man the centre of your universe. In my case, somehow, that had never happened. Call it providence or a safeguard valve, God had used to protect me from totally breaking down, but that is what it was. From the very start, I never had a chance to fall in love with my husband. Yes, he was very dear to me and I loved him. But I was not *in* love with him. He always kept himself at a distance from me and that is what saved me. In many ways, he was a stranger. Again, that may sound unrealistic but it was the truth. What else would you call a person who though living with you, sleeping with you (on the odd occasion or enough to produce one son), eating with you and spending evenings with you going out (hardly ever alone) but never knew your innermost thoughts, your pain or things that made you happy. Why you cried when listening to a particular song or why you got into a bad mood when watching a particular movie. He did not have a clue, nor an inkling. He was your husband in name and you were his for the world but the intimacy, the softness, the love that was supposed to be there was missing.

Well, that is what saved me. I did not break down like another woman might have and today although I do not have a man in my life, I do have a wonderful son. I am no longer searching for why I didn't make him happy. I know why and with that answer has come a kind of peace. I hope one day I will find that special person who will light up my life the way I had dreamed all those years ago. I have not found him yet and although I am still waiting, I am not unhappy. If it happens there is nothing else I could wish for and if it does not, well, there are worse ways to live one's life.

When Avinash came to say goodbye, I was having a bath. He told the maid to tell me he was waiting outside. I took my time. I soaped my body as never before; sometimes two, three times behind my knees and under my elbows. I was not planning to wash my hair but I decided just as I put the soap down and stood with the water falling on me, that it was dirty. Two washes were essential and after that I had to wait for the conditioner to do its magic before I could wash it out.

I towelled myself dry with exaggerated care but then wore my clothes as if a fire had just broken out. Although I wanted to make Avinash suffer and this small gesture gave me some momentary satisfaction, I now felt small and mean. This was not really my style. I hoped he had not left and felt a small thrill of relief when I saw him sitting in what used to be our bedroom living-room.

He took my face in his hands which were warm against the cool of my face and stared deep into my eyes. Both of us were crying softly and then he kissed me on my lips. It was a soft kiss; chaste and loving. "I love you, Arundhati. Look after yourself and please, please forgive me."

I did not mean to but I broke down then. I put my arms tightly around his neck and hugged him for a long long time. There were no words, nothing could be said to describe the pain and heartbreak that gripped us. Our silence said it all. "Goodbye dear husband, dear friend. Goodbye to what I thought was a marriage and a love that was. We would start again, he would be my best friend and I would always be there for him." I knew his thoughts mirrored mine. We smiled through our tears and then he was gone.

15

Avinash moved towards the balcony and stood looking at the lush greenery without really seeing any of its beauty. His thoughts once again turned to Arundhati.

She listened to me without a murmur as I went on baring my soul. At the end of it, she took my hand in hers and said very clearly: "Life doesn't always fulfil our expectations, does it? It beckons us and captivates us but when we succumb it plunges its dagger without remorse, with precise skill and cruelty. I understand exactly what you mean." And I knew that she did *indeed* understand what I meant. I was so glad she did not come out with a sympathetic though meaningless platitude. That is not what I wanted to hear. This was. I didn't want hushed whispers, boring inanities and sympathetic murmurings. I needed someone to understand what I was feeling and to agree that yes, life was difficult and unjust and that I had every right to feel the way I was feeling. Looking at her, I felt a lot of my anger and misery dissipate.

We were talking in the garden but I had stopped noticing anything except her beauty. She was smiling bravely at me from beneath her long lashes and her rosy lips were enchanting in their fullness. I cursed myself for hurting such beauty, such delicate beauty. All at once, everything appeared oppressive and I wished I could press my body against hers and forget the pain I had caused her.

She really understood. I was not at fault, maybe neither one of us was but I was just glad that someone else realised it. At that moment I knew we had transcended our marriage and replaced it with the first blossomings of friendship.

Arundhati's mother-in-law passed by her with a group of *chamchis*. Neither looked at each other.

My mother-in-law was aghast when she heard the news but refused to break down in front of me. She stood by Avinash stoicly. She was the upper crust who never betrayed their feelings and instead heaped the blame on me for turning her precious son to other men.

My mother-in-law was extremely direct. "I must tell you," she said at her imperious best, "that I blame you entirely for this mess. You should have prevented this from coming out in the open. He is your husband after all and you have to take the good with the bad."

I found her remarks insensitive and cruel and as always her refusal to see the truth and her obvious hatred of me touched a core of me so deep I knew I would never speak to her again and I never did.

What is it, what is it with women that makes them both ferocious and gentle? Why are they their own worst enemies? My mother-in-law had shown great affection towards me before I got married. Once the deed was actually done, her attitude changed dramatically. She made me feel like an intruder, she did not trust me and from the very first day she made it clear that the house was hers and that I was to have nothing to do with its daily functioning. She was no longer affectionate but displayed a cool manner towards me. Any action on my part was treated with disdain and indifference. She was always watching me, willing me to make a gaffe or faux pas so that she or the other members of her family could put me in my place. And why all this resentment? Simply because I had married her son? I however soon realised it wasn't something personal. It could have been someone else in my place and the situation would have been the same.

Mrs Arundhati Diwan looked at Arundhati seated on the swing and Avinash standing alone and aloof.

There was never any inkling that Avinash was different. He fulfilled all the requirements of a son one could be proud of and as he grew up, I thought we were good buddies. We played tennis and chess often, exchanged notes on work and general topics such as politics, the environment, some play or the other and sports. But I realise it was a safe relationship. Neither of us delved too deeply into the unknown realms of the other. I thought I knew him but I did not know him at all. My son has become a stranger after years of living in close proximity to each other, I find we are after all, not really close.

Arundhati looked down at the garden swing. It was quite beautiful. It was actually an intricately carved patterned tomb-shaped minaret, that blended with the mystery of the garden. She kicked off her shoes. They fell to the floor upright. The woman next to her looked at the shoes and almost fell forward in an attempt to read the label. She had bought her shoes at one of the most exclusive shops in New York. The lady sat still for a few minutes and then did something very strange. She took off her shoes with exaggerated casualness pressing her feet with her hands as if they were hurting.

Arundhati looked at her shoes with no hidden motives and naturally could not help but see the label. It was an equally exclusive design. The woman noticed she had noticed and with a smug look on her face barely concealing her triumph, she put her shoes on, all the earlier drama cast aside, and with a look that said, "I too am part of the exclusive club" walked inside.

These inane gestures were part of the rich people's world and Arundhati was used to it. Most people who belonged to this group were insecure and shallow and needed these little games to prove they were richer which was synonymous with better, than others.

Rajeev, my beloved son, came up to me looking very grown-up in his new suit and bow-tie. He wasn't normally allowed to attend parties but the host's son was a school-friend and they were only going to be here for an hour. After that he would go back home.

I might not have given in to his entreaties to attend the party but the blow with Avinash had left him feeling low and somehow displaced. I understood that and felt there was no harm in spoiling him a little.

16

Rajeev was a tiny baby. He weighed just under six pounds. But what he lacked in weight he more than made up in manner. Right from the beginning, he was an active and alert child. He was extremely hairy and I took to calling him my little gorilla. At first, I had been worried about the facial hair but I was told it would soon disappear and after a few months his pudgy cheeks came into full display.

It was a difficult birth and I was in labour for almost twenty-two hours. All through that time, I cursed and shouted wondering why I had to go through this terrible pain. But when I saw my son, I never questioned that agony again. I loved him from the moment I set eyes on him. Right through my pregnancy, I had wondered at this new life I was carrying within me and had felt great pangs of affection each time he kicked or moved inside me. But nothing prepared me for the overwhelming feeling of intense love that overcame me on holding him in my arms. I felt nothing else mattered any more. All the pain and worry that had consumed my daily attention faded into insignificance. Nothing mattered any more, nothing but my son.

That this squashed little bundle, this tiny little person that had come out of me could evoke such powerful emotions came as a complete surprise. And yet deep down, I had known how it would be all along.

When he opened his eyes and looked at me as if to say "yes, you are my mother," I felt a piercing shaft move from my throat to my heart where it lodged itself, growing in intensity with every passing second.

Every little smile, a gurgle or pucker, a frown or even when he cried would find me in responding emotions alternating between despair and fear or great joy and well being.

"Look, look at him smile," I would tell Avinash, for he was a sunny child and was always good natured. Avinash was a good father which I initially resented. I couldn't help it. I wanted Rajeev all to myself. I was also slightly bitter, after all if he was not a very good husband I had thought the same trend would continue with fatherhood. But he proved otherwise.

Towards the end of my pregnancy, when I was huge and weighed down, he had been extremely attentive. But there was no indication of the transformation that was to take place. He would come home early and sometimes stop by even during the day. He loved to bathe him, feed him and even change his nappies. No task was too much for him. He was so unlike himself or maybe he became more like himself in Rajeev's company, I was not really sure. But it was good to see him like this. He could spend hours cooing and whispering to him. I never knew how good a storyteller he was till I heard him weave some fantastic tales together. It reminded me of my childhood spent in the awning of Amah's storytelling and I was glad Rajeev would grow up with an equally rich heritage.

Rajeev was an only child and extremely intuitive. He worshipped his mother and being the only child they were naturally close. He learnt her moods and knew when she was happy and sad. These emotions were always connected to his father, someone whom he loved dearly but was not very close to because he was always away on some business or the other but also because as he grew older the time they spent together lessened.

After this particular argument which I think the whole

household heard, perhaps not the exact words but certainly the voices raised in anger; the shouting and crying my mother came to wish good-night as she always did.

It was ten-thirty when she tapped on the door and came in.

She never concealed anything from me, indeed it would have been pointless to do so. "I hope you are not too upset," she said, taking me in her arms without waiting for a reply.

"I'm sorry you had such a bad fight with papa," I said, a few minutes later.

She kissed me lovingly and pushed my hair back from my forehead. "It's not your fault. Forget about it. Do not worry so much, all right?" At fourteen, there were many things I could do. I knew how to repair a bicycle or fix a blown fuse. But I could not fix what was very wrong now. I acquiesced, and as she smiled at me, I noticed she was looking particularly beautiful. Beautiful and sad. As a child I had always taken my mother's beauty for granted, indeed I had never paid any attention. It was the way she was, it just seemed so natural. I couldn't imagine her any other way. But tonight as I was leaving my childhood behind, I began to see her beauty with new and wiser eyes. She was in her late thirties, though she did not look it at all. One was instantly arrested by her hair, long and black and luxurious with a perpetual sheen to it. Her skin wasn't the browny sallow colour most Indian women seemed to have. Her's was creamy with a touch of the rose in it. Her eyes were wide and long lashed, their colour changing constantly depending on her emotion. Now they were a deep brown which happened when she was very emotional. Her figure was perfect, I knew that by now and I felt a great surge of love and protection for her as I marvelled at this woman who meant so much to me.

I wanted so much to help her and as she bade me good-night I clung to her fervently, wishing I could make her smile and make everything all right.

I knew things were not fine between my parents. I had known that for a long time. You cannot live in the same house and be totally oblivious to what's happening around you. Initially they had tried not to have arguments when I was around but as the years went by, I guess the situation got worse and although they never said anything negative to each other in my presence, you could hear their raised voices in the next room.

As far back as I can remember, I have loved my mother. She meant everything to me. She was gentle, kind and understanding. We seemed to have a bond between us that did not exist with my father. Don't get me wrong, I loved him dearly but we weren't as close. We didn't really spend time together and in a way we did not really know each other. He was not there the first time I went to school, or had my first fight or my first teenage feelings about my lack of self-confidence. He wasn't there to answer all those unfathomable questions that children come up with, to put me to bed or hold me when I just needed to be held.

Some of the best times my mother and I had together were in the kitchen. I loved to watch my mother baking in the kitchen. One by one the ingredients – sugar, butter, eggs and flour – would disappear. Her usually immaculate hair had wisps sticking out and there was a thin sheen of sweat on her face. There would be bits of cake-mix on her clothes and face and I loved helping her wipe it off. She would give me the cloth and tell me to do my job, but that was at the end. Initially the aroma of the cake would spread through the whole house and leave me with a great sense of happiness and well-being. By the time she had finished mixing the cake-mix, my mouth would be watering in anticipation and I would rush to the mixing bowl to scrape some of the cake-mix which I knew my mother would have left for me. That was the beginning of the fun. At first I would eat quickly as if I had never tasted the cake mixture before pushing my chubby fingers around the rim and scooping big dripping portions on the tip of my finger. After the first few fingers, I would slow down realising from past experience the mixture was almost half finished. My pace would get slower and slower and all too soon I was licking a clean bowl. My mother would eventually take the bowl from me telling me to leave some place for the cake. At this I would brighten up and just manage to contain my anticipation with the heavenly smell wafting from the oven.

Thus, it was natural I should feel closer to my mother. But it wasn't only that. At times when I tried to be objective, I could see what a fabulous person she was apart from being a mother. She instilled in me the right values and helped differentiate between right and wrong. So, although I never really knew the nature of the problem between the two of them, I instinctively sided with my mother. She could do no wrong.

One might say I was abnormally sensitive to every nuance of my mother's behaviour.

17

Many parents believe there are some topics which are taboo for their children and hence never to be spoken about. But in this age of satellite television it would indeed be difficult if not downright impossible for children not to learn about certain matters of their own accord. Sex was one of them. My mother never talked to me about matters such as these and although she was forthright and practical, I suspect she was too embarrassed to ever broach the subject. But I never thought of it that way. My child needed to know about his father's preference and I had to explain it to him in the best possible manner. He also needed to be told by me rather than hear it from someone else.

By the time Avinash told me his sad secet, my son was already a quietly self-possessed human being who knew more than he should. I think because he was an only child he read a lot more and spending time with adults, had grown up quickly. At the age of fourteen, he knew all the facts and dissimilated them in a manner that was comfortable for him. Hence when I called him to the study he walked in casually, sat down and looked at me enquiringly, for a moment I was at a loss for words.

I did not want to give him a lecture on right or wrong, each is different for different people. Nor did I think there was anything wrong in Avinash's choice, what I found wrong was his marrying me knowing where his preferences lay. That was wrong. And he was certainly no babe in the woods when he married me so he should have known better.

I had been brought up to believe that sex before

marriage was wrong but I personally didn't subscribe to that view. I did think that hopping out of one bed to the other was wrong. But what if I had a daughter, how does a mother tell her innocent and doe-eyed daughter that it is acceptable. Will she understand what you are saying or plunge head-long into an affair instantly taking off her clothes for any man? I sighed deeply to myself. Being a parent was so difficult in this day and age. I am sure my mother didn't have to face these additional problems.

"There is a huge disparity between what one should do and what one does," I said. "What," I continued, "I want to say is how you should conduct yourself when you have to face this gap." I knew I was being evasive and Rajeev often patient and considerate paid no heed to my obvious hesitation. "Hurry up mama, I can't understand what you are saying at all. Not at all."

I started talking as calmly as I could while he listened attentively. By the time I had finished he looked quite sick and I tried to take him in my arms but he brushed me aside and said: "Do you mean to tell me dad's gay?" He then blushed scarlet and looked if anything more miserable. I felt terrible and cursed Avinash for putting us in this position. And I could understand his son's searing pain, after all, and we were talking about his father, someone he loved very much, this wasn't an inanimate discussion.

After the terrible news my mother had given me, I felt quite ill but I hid it from her because I knew she would worry and fuss over me. I didn't want that. I needed to be on my own and think about all the things she had talked about. I knew what gay meant. I had looked it up in the dictionary. Apart from meaning merry and cheerful, it also meant homosexual. I had heard the term "homo" at school. It was used by the older boys when they talked about Mr Khurana who was our biology teacher. He walked in a funny kind of way and was always giggling stupidly. My father was not at all like him and I wondered what the two had in common.

I lay awake all night thinking of my father.

He had come to me that evening looking tired and defeated. And yet, yet there was a sense of peace about him. He told me all about himself, things I didn't really understand but they sounded right and I felt he had a need to unburden himself. He talked quietly and calmly but with the passion of conviction as if he knew he was finally doing something right.

He admitted he was wrong. Wrong from the very beginning. He had lacked the courage to stand up against his mother and his numerous relatives who made him their business after he returned from America. He should never have married but in doing so and in going along with the marriage he had perpetuated his crime. He even admitted that though he had great feelings for my mother, he could never give her the love a husband should. He had ruined her life and that's what he felt most miserable about. He was telling me all this, he said, because he hoped in time I would understand. There was no point in lying any more or living the lie any more. He just hoped they would continue to be friends after this.

We were both crying by the time he finished and although a part of me hated him for what he was and what he had done, another part of me understood the burden he had been carrying and I suddenly thought, "well, it's brave of him to tell me all this face to face. A lot of fathers might not have done the same thing."

When he left, I though of all the times we had spent together. They weren't many but still they meant a lot to me. I remembered the time we had gone fishing and he had netted a huge salmon. We were both ecstatic. "Papa, you are the greatest," I had exclaimed in joy and he had hugged me and laughingly replied: "I'm not that great, son. I'm not that great."

I cried quietly in my bed feeling a great sense of sadness and loss. I was happy to be staying with my mother. I wouldn't have wanted it any other way, but still the reality of our changed lives overwhelmed me.

Although the party was far from over, in fact, guests were still arriving, Amah came to tell Rajeev it was time to leave. He was talking to Avinash and both looked visibly upset. I moved towards them hoping to avert a scene if possible. I knew that Rajeev was going through an especially harrowing time but I have nothing to worry as Amah takes him firmly in hand and with a look at me she whisks him away.

18

Whenever I feel low and depressed about the way things have turned out, I think of Amah and am instantly grateful for what I have. Amah was married when she was still a child playing with her dolls and sitting o her father's lap. She was only six. She does not remember anything; the ceremonial fire and the smoke that rose and threatened to engulf, the heavy chanting and the sonorous words of the priest, her bridegroom who was somewhat older than she was who looked on with feigned disdain though he was also too young to understand the machinations of his elders.

When she became a woman, she was sent to her in-laws' house. Although her mother-in-law had been in favour of the match, she didn't treat her well from the start. She took her gold ornaments and few saris from her saying she would lock them away in her steel closet. But after a few weeks, she began using the jewellery and saris. Amah protested to her husband who only went and told his mother who in turn made life hell for her.

Her daily routine was one of extreme drudgery. She woke at five in the morning, cleaned the house, washed the clothes and made sure there was enough water for everyone's baths. She barely managed to dip herself in the village stream before she was back at the house to make breakfast. After the men-folk had left for the fields, she was left with her mother-in-law who sat herself in the verandah from where she issued orders.

On top of everything else, she remained barren. It was not the son's fault, he was every night grunting loudly and pushing between her thighs. But after a few years and the constant examination of her belly, It became apparent that there was to be no child. She was thrown out of the house and told to return to where she had come from.

Amah could not bear the shame and ignominy of going back to her parents and she ventured forth into the big city where she drifted from job to job as a domestic servant eventually coming to work with our family.

From the moment I set eyes on her, I was enslaved. She is all that a woman should be: tough though pliant, strong though understanding and, above all, gentle and feminine. She makes most people look clumsy with her graciousness. Especially when it comes to eating. For eating with one's hands is really a messy task with bits of rice falling off your hands and *dal* running down your arms. The yoghurt is sometimes slurped directly attended by loud noises and the finale is the belch accorded greatness because it indicates satisfaction at the meal consumed.

Amah was the perfect eater. She had elevated eating to the level of art. She took her time and never wolfed her food down as the other servants did ravenous after a day's hard work. She would survey her food impassively and then make small near perfect balls of her rice, *dal* and vegetables. They would all be tumbled together and slipped unobstrusively, in the blink of an eyelid into her mouth. Often, if I did not concentrate, I would miss out on this crucial bit. She ate noiselessly and before you knew it she was drinking her water which signalled the end of her meal. It took me years of practice before I perfected Amah's art of eating. It amused me no end to overhear at a party a comment on my eating habits, that 'it was the *khandaani* way!'

I often look at her as she goes about her chores, empty like a shell. Her skin is lined with wrinkles each having a story to tell. Her eyes are dry and unfathomable for she has no more tears to shed. Grief clings to her like a second skin but still she moves with dignity and I see in her carriage great courage for all she has lost and the life that stretches before her devoid of any great joy or real happiness.

Amah could feel Arundhati's eyes bore into her back as she takes Rajeev away. She sighs inaudibly thinking how much this "almost daughter" is suffering.

I feel Arundhati's pain intensely. She is like a daughter to me and when she suffers, I suffers. But although the pain feels like it will never go away, it will. I speak from experience.

19

When I arrived at my husband's house, I must have looked like a divine gift from the gods. I was a tall girl, big built so I looked older than my thirteen years. I had cried when my parents had told me where we were going but I had seen many young girls leave their houses and knew nothing could change my lot. I carried my childhood companions with me; the doll my father had bought me at a travelling *mela*, the dresses my mother had sewn for my doll saving precious material that we could ill afford. My little *potli* contained a picture book I loved looking at that was badly torn and whose pages were well thumbed and crumpled and a snow-white handkerchief embroidered with lace. My mother had also sent three saris and a few small pieces of jewellery.

My link with my past lay in those little pieces of memory and I cherished each and every one of them. But before long my mother-in-law had thrown away the doll saying I was too old, the hanky, saris and jewellery were now her own while my book was torn to shreds by her cruel and merciless hands.

I remember that day clearly. The sun was ferocious in its intensity. Day after day of sweltering heat that wrings that sweat from my body in tiny rivulets that go zigagging and disappear into nothingness.

I would massage my mother-in-law's body and then after my husband had had his way with me would sit well into the night pressing his legs. It was not much of an existence.

Even in my own house things changed after I got married. Now I belonged to another family. "Narayan's bride looks tired today," my mother would say when I came back from the fields, or "how lucky Malavati is, look at her and see how big and strong she has become. She will bring good luck to her new house." My mother did not refer to me like this because she did not love me but she was giving in to superstition that said you should not covet what is no longer yours. By continually referring to me as belonging to someone else, she was appeasing the gods. I hated being referred to as someone else's wife or daughter but I had no choice but to listen, for customs change slowly especially in the villages and once a bargain had been struck there was no going back.

At times, when my mother made me do chores I did not want to, I would yell out angrily saying I was happy I was going to my new house. But those words were far from the truth. I was terrified of leaving my parents but my mother would only answer back in the affirmative and say she was glad which made it even worse. Because I was hiding my true feelings and hurting both my mother and myself.

My family lived in a small mud hut that my father's father had built. It was the only thing we could call our own. The land which we tilled was mortgaged and we never seemed to be able to pay off more than the interest that accrued every year. We barely had enough to eat and it was always the same diet of *chapati* and *dal* and on luckier days we could look forward to a vegetable. We were better off than most for we had a buffalo and some chickens. But both the milk and the eggs were sold to make ends meet.

We tolled from morning to night and often it was backbreaking labour with the heat pounding down ceaselessly and mercilessly upon us. The best times I can remember were always by the river which ran through the village. It was a dirty river full of floating debris, weeds and human faeces but sometimes the water would turn from dark brown to blue-green and we would jump into the water with gay abandon.

During the rainy season the water would swell, the waves would pound against the floating debris that lapped against the tangled beds of water hyacinths. I loved to watch the birds on rare occasions swoop down from the great height above and catch a fish in the running water.

Once we even caught a fish, a rarity, for these slippery creatures refused to swim in the murky water. What a day it was, we were ecstatic, shouting and jumping for joy. And when we cooked it with specially pounded *masalas,* I thought I would never be so happy again. Even eating it never measured up to the happiness I experienced before.

I saw my husband sitting across from me in his father's lap looking surly even though he was dressed in all his finery. He was a fat boy and now and then he was moved from various relatives but he almost came back to his father, I'm sure much to his dismay.

My in-laws were far better off than us. They had a real house made of cement and a tiled roof. There was even a courtyard which showed they had money to spend on luxuries. When I arrived, I was told to quickly change out of the bright red *ghagra choli* my mother had scrimped and saved for and made to wear an old dirty bundle and pushed into the kitchen. That was the beginning of my new life and I realised all my fears were not unfounded.

I met my husband after a few days because there were guests in the house and an extra pair of hands was needed in the kitchen. One night I was lying on the floor staring at the stars and wondering if they looked the same back home when I felt an enormous hairy hand touch my things. I screamed out in fright only to be rudely slapped and told to keep quiet. It wasn't an auspicious beginning.

Between the long nights with my husband who had turned out to be far more spoiled than when I had seen him on his father's lap all those years ago and even longer days at my mother-in-law's beck and call, I had no time to think, to wonder if I was happy, to think of my parents or even wish for anything. Any blows I received and pain I suffered I began to think was because I was at fault. They had wiped out my desire to live and I went from one day to the other listening to their commands and adhering to them in total passivity. My mother-in-law was difficult and demanding and my initial rebellion was soon snuffed out. Thus, I learnt how to be a dutiful wife and daughter. I could iron clothes so well that even the creases felt ashamed to appear and I cleaned the house so meticulously that not a speck of dust dared show its face. I knew if the chicken was adequately spiced, the meat tender and the fish well marinated even with my eyes closed. Though I now ate food I didn't know existed, I would have gladly traded it all for the simple *chapati* and *dal* at my parents' home.

20

Arundhati watched Amah and Rajeev as they walked away. She turned towards Avinash.

His height was accentuated by the loss of weight. There were deep lines running from his nose to his mouth. His eyes were dark and unfathomable, he had cloaked his pain, not allowing me to see the terrible ravage it had wrought. I saw a touch of silver at his temples and a rush of tender love shot through me. I could not blame him any longer. His shoulders were drooping from the burden and I was worried it might prove too much for him. I would not add to that. After all, we had found friendship together and would always be joined together by our son.

Avinash has left. I am alone like I have always been. I sit by myself as the world goes about its business. The words I have written stare back at me. They act as a panacea for my loss and will I know, with time, goad me on. Disappointment is a reflection of only one part of my feelings, for my emotions are constantly shifting as I remember different pasts of my life.

The brimming of hope
laid aside
to rest asunder
the plight to hide
the teardrops glisten
and now they fall
delicate, imbalance
dewdrops of the morn

I learnt to love Avinash even though he is not what I wanted. I grew up dreaming of someone else. Everything about him was wrong for me. It is like the jigsaw puzzle that does not fit. And then you find that your time is up. When my time had come none of the pieces had matched the visions, the many expectations I had lived so long with. And, yet, I had loved him. I had also chosen him knowingly. I married him without coercion. Although my parents had not really delved into my reasons, I cannot say that they tied my hands or whipped me to the ceremonious pyre *a la* Hindi movie tragedies. I did it all myself. Perhaps not fully understanding the situation but certainly aware of what was happening around me and to me.

I have learnt that one can love someone and yet not love him at the same time simply because he is not what you want. It is not a pleasant situation to be in because one's emotions are constantly playing havoc with them. You are always justifying and explaining to yourself. There is a nagging feeling of having less than, and to live with that feeling day in and day out is crushing.

The party had stretched itself in all directions and showed no signs of slowing down. Outside the skies were dark and cloudy, their anger palpable as they roared out loudly and lit up the heavens with ruthless velocity. The trees swayed from side to side in complete abandon, while the flowers had no choice but to droop in submission against the onslaught of incessant rain. It lasted all night but the first rays of dawn brought another picture. There was the smell of fresh mud and a gentle breeze played with my hair as I bent to pick up a flower. A calmness pervaded the air, and a sense of peace reigned as if the sky god had been appeased.

TARA

21

It was difficult to explain, let alone make one understand the terrifying feeling of abandonment and the creeping up on one of old age. When a woman is no longer young, she suffers dreadful insecurity, a terror of ageing and a sure knowledge that without her good looks she will no longer appeal to her partner. Especially when one moved in such circles where in a sense the chase was on perpetually and the younger the woman, the more virile a man felt. The more envious his friends would feel. But the younger ones were fickle and would dump their old mate as soon as new pastures beckoned. You see they were no better than the man. As we all know, we live in extremely debauched times.

My name is Tara, which means star and for my mother I was the bright star in her life. My father left us when I was a few days old and as I obviously have no recollection of him he never left an impression on my life.

I was born in a squalid flat which smelt of stale air and rotten garbage. By the time I was five, we moved to another flat which was only slightly better because it was right next to a market. So, we had the rotten garbage, the snell of fried food and *mithai* from the neighbouring *halwai* to break the monotony.

The air is always heavy and humid. It is a mixture of man's sweat and his filth, animals, cooking, flowers and incense. The atmosphere is oppressive but the heat continues to wither those who stay too long in its path. The roads are melting, the ground is dry and arid, gasping for water. There is no gentle breeze to soothe our skins but plenty of mosquitoes that feed on our blood. The birds make a token appearance but their cries are muted and they soon withdraw to the shade of a solitary tree.

When we moved into the flat, apart from the smell, we also inherited Aunty Verma.

Aunty Verma and my mother were the best of friends and also the worst of enemies. They lived in the same locality and their flats adjoined each other. They spent their entire lives comparing each other's clothes, shoes, crockery, linen, servants and since everything was dissected between them, even their children. Both had daughters born around the same time. But Mala was a few minutes older than me and those few minutes gave her the advantage and it seemed for the rest of my life that she held on to those few minutes with great tenacity.

So, we grew up being constantly compared. It began with our baby features; our little feet and cute belly buttons, who yelled the loudest and who spoke first. The clothes we outgrew and the stains we put on them. And then it was Mala's first star, her prizes, her scholarship, her studies abroad, her job and her marriage. Somewhere along the way, the comparison with me no longer mattered and I was dropped, only to be picked up now and then to further prove some point in her favour.

How my mother hated those odious comparisons and how she would shrivel up when she saw Aunty Verma coming up the front door. She had no defences against her though she did put up a fight in the beginning. She made me join classical singing classes since I had shown an interest in the great *ghazal* singers. The mellifluous voice of Farida Khanum, the throaty Mehdi Hassan and the unique Ghulam Ali.Usted Fateh Ali Khan's singing could keep me enrapt for hours as did the instrumental music of the Indian greats – Pandit Shiv Kumar Sharma, Amjad Ali Khan and Bismillah Khan. However, this move proved embarrassing. I was pronounced tone deaf with a voice that would never amount to anything. Next I tried painting. Indian art was seeing a revival and the rise in prices, plus the rave reviews of even the mediocre, convinced her it could prove to be my forte. The attempt at painting was dismal and I was actually asked to leave the class, my drawings considered no better than a three-year-old! My mother made one last attempt, so great was her desire to stem Aunty Verma's onslaught. The new apron and cook's hat that were meant to "put us in the mood" were perfect as were the cooking utensils and other apparatus. What was not perfect was my performance. Nothing turned out right. The simplest of vegtables became a great chore. Green ladies-fingers turned charcoal black, innocent-looking brinjal turned into an unmentionable mush and rice, the safest of dishes was either overdone and watery or uncooked and tough. Baking exotic souffles, lemon meringues and all butter madeira cakes were equally dismaying. They never seemed to rise high enough or the consistency was incorrect and hence they were totally unappealing. I suffering greatly when my dish was put alongside the other superb looking extravaganzas that seemed to have been put together effortlessly. I gave up then and so did my mother.

There was no time to be idle as I grew up. My mother was not a strict disciplinarian, more a benevolent one which meant that while she did not push me constantly to do household chore, nevertheless they had to be done. We had a maid who came in the morning to wash the clothes and sweep the floors but other than that we did the rest of the chores ourselves. The *dhobi* round the corner ironed the clothes but I can still remember times when money was tight and we had to forgo that luxury. My mother was an indifferent cook but knew how to stretch a vegetable so it could be used for two meals instead of one. My clothes were good quality bought from street hawkers who managed to lay their hands on export rejects. That way we saved on the fancy overheads and yet managed to wear clothes that we were not ashamed of.

I was often asked about my father. "Where is your father?"

"He has gone abroad."

From an early age, I realised that not having a father was some kind of sin. So I used this answer to cover up. I had heard about "abroad." It was where fortunate people went because the land was green and beautiful and the air was clean. There were hundreds of different birds and plants and lots of delicious things to eat.

When Aunty Verma's daughter, Mala, heard me say this she was very put out. But she soon got to know the truth and made life unbearable for me and that's when we had a horrible fight and I decided I hated her for destroying the illusion I had begun to believe and that allowed me to live in some semblance of peace without a father.

I remember being called all kinds of names when I was growing up. Its something you never forget. I needed braces for my front two teeth and from being called bugs bunny I was then known as stainless steel. Although I was dark, I had a fairly good skin but during my teenage years, I suddenly developed two huge pimples on either side of my cheeks in exactly the same position (I measured them out with a mixture of disgust and curiosity) and was thereafter called twin peaks. Later as the pimples spread all over my face, I was called spotted dick, lifted from the name of a delicious sponge cake filled with sultanas!

Over the years, I began to hate the penny pinching, the look of poverty that hung over our flat despite our best attempts and the sly and malevolent looks of Aunty Verma and her daughter.

In my imaginings, I did everything perfectly. I was exquisite and no matter what Aunty Verma said and the teachers who turned me away from their classes, I never doubted my ability to perfect everything.

My childhood and teens had seen my mother's disappointed face weave itself in and out of my waking and sleeping hours. Soon I got so used to seeing her disappointment that I took it for granted. Having said that I also have to admit that a little bit of me continued to die inside each time I saw her face raised in expectation at the start of a new venture only to be replaced by defeat at the end.

I never measured up to my mother's expectations. I always fell short no matter how hard I tried. Too much of this and too little of that. I often felt like a dish she was cooking and despite her adding all the right ingredients there was still something missing.

It is difficult to talk to my mother about anything because the moment I try to say something, she becomes defensive and launches into a full-scale attack. She seems to have all the answers. Most of our conversations went something like this.

"Mama, can I talk to you for a moment?" She was always sitting with Aunty Verma in the small balcony outside our living room listening mostly in silence to her praise her daughter but now and then it would become too much for my mother and then she would try valiantly to rise to the occasion and say something positive about me.

She came in at once. She always liked to believe we were friends who understood each other. I looked at her in exasperation wanting to tell her off for fibbing about me.

But before I could say anything, she pulled me aside into the kitchen and launched into a long monologue. "What does Aunty Verma and her silly daughter know? You, you are going to do something good and show them what colours you are made of. What colours I have given you. There are so many different hues inside you and you have only tried out a few. So, so," she raised her shoulders and hands and shrugged nonchalantly, "the classes did not work out, so you didn't suit each other but it will happen you will see, they all will see." She moved back towards the balcony and then turned, "did you want to say something?" I just shook my head and anyway what was the point?

I would often stare at myself in the bedroom mirror and talk to my reflection. "Why," I asked myself, "did I have to be so ordinary? Why did I not have even one quality that could redeem me in the eyes of my mother?" I would often end these nightly sessions by crying which made me look even uglier and the last image I saw before I went to bed was this dark face with an angry scowl and swollen eyes.

When my mother prodded me to attend these classes, we would have our many argunments. I would be sullen and resentful, scared of failing her again and would yell in desperation, "why should I go to these stupid classes? You know I'm no good, I'll never be better than Mala."

She would stand in front of me and just stare. She never said anything. She would just stare and stare and force me into saying something. She wuld make me feel so guilty that I would finally acquiesce.

It was during one of these nightly sessions that I came across the other me. I was crying as usual when I saw my image dissolve and take a new form. This other me was laughing and sure of herself. She did not care what other people said about her because they didn't know her, the real her. That was the beginning of the new me. I kept it within me promising that one day I would show them all and wipe the sneer off Aunty Verma's face. When I married Rohit and moved to my new house I knew there was no time to waste. The inner me told me it was time to show the world what I was made of. "Any more delays," it said, "and then you will really be nothing."

22

There were people huddled into little groups everywhere as it usually is at parties. But there was one crowd which was larger than usual. The laughter was louder and the words were meant to be heard. I looked to see what was so interesting about the group and realised the moment I got to its fringes.

Sheila was as usual the cynosure of all eyes with her husband throwing in a remark now and then. But with a perpetual glass of something in hand he had nothing really to say. It was just a meaningless charade to grab some attention. It happened repeatedly at each party, where his wife was the crowd puller. He was the big industrialist but it was his wife that called the shots. So, people fawned on her, admiring her clothes, her jewellery, her hair, whatever they could. If she deigned to talk to you, you could later say you knew her and intersperse your conversation with quotes from her. "Sunita was saying..." or "you know Sunita, so and so person." It was all part of the society game and a lot of humbug.

I saw Aunty Verma looking around for a chair and when no one obliged, she got into her act. Aunty Verma is short and at times bends all the way over so that her heavy bosom and thick midriff become one. Her thin spindly legs look bent from the weight above and always appear as if they are just going to cave in. Needless to say that never happened but it was an illusion she worked on to get lifts and help carry her groceries and when she wanted a chair at a party.

I do not know how she was named Shanti for she had a bad temper which manifested itself in the flared nostrils and the children in the locality swore they saw fire emerge from them like a dragon!

I hated Aunty Verma. She had more influence in our home than my mother and her approval or disapproval hung in the air long after she had left for the day.

She did not resort to frontal attack. No, she would worm and wiggle her way into the camp and before you were aware of it, wham! She would hit. She would do this again and again till she had demolished her opponent.

She did this quietly. She would not say anything at first. Then just when you thought you were home free she would begin the onslaught. She would toss out a small remark, it would hit its target but not enough the person. She even gave them enough time to stand up and regain some semblance of equilibrium before the next dart was pitched forward. The intervals between each remark were being blitzed from all sides. You had to take cover before it was too late. You wriggled frantically forward, searching for something to hang on, to take you out of this onslaught but the enemy was merciless. She had sounded you out and till she had quashed you like a fly there would be no relief.

When Rohit and his parents had come to visit me at our house, we were privy to one of her attacks.

Tara's mother, simple and dignified, watched the encounter as if a guest. Aunty Verma had taken charge of affairs and was presiding over the meeting in her usual pompous manner. The whole *mohalla* knew about the evening and naturally Aunty Verma was there dressed for the special occasion so that they mistook her for the bride's mother. That pleased her no end for my mother was dressed in a simple silk sari her usual party pearls on display. But

Aunty Verma had on a bright bordered sari, flowers in her hair and more jewellery than both of us possessed. When I bravely told her she was too dressed up, she said someone had to make up for the two of us.

Rohit was a tall man, almost six feet in his stockinged feet but he had a slight stoop. He was hairy and the third open button on his shirt testified that. He had a permanent smile on his face and also laughed easily. He played golf at weekends and swam in the morning at the local club before going to work. There were a few awkward pauses during tea that usually happen on occasions like this and Roit tried to cover those silences with a few jokes and funny remarks.

Aunty Verma saw this whole situation in a totally different light. Rohit was hunch-backed. He was a *badmaash* because he kept his buttons open like any local *goonda*. He smiled too easily which meant he had something to hide and you could see he didn't brush his teeth at night because they were yellowish. Since he spent so much time at sports he would never be a success at his work because his mind was obviously somewhere else. He was crude because his jokes were in bad taste thus showing poor judgement. He had failed in Aunty Verma's opinion and she refused to back down from her verdict.

For the first time my mother stood up against her and said she liked what she had seen and if the boy accepted the match she was going to say "yes." I don't know where she got the courage to go against that thunderous brow, the thin set lips and blackened eyes, but she did. She found the resolve from somewhere.

Why had she ever allowed Aunty Verma to have a strong influence on her, to enter her life and its private domain and let her be privy to every little fear, every little problem, I never really understood. My mother was a weak and timid person who lost her husband very early in life. Today, we barely managed to scrape a living together from my father's pension. It seemed all the life had been squeezed out of her like a dried up lemon and when she met Aunty Verma, well, she just let her take over. In a sense she became my mother's surrogate husband. It was a sad story but both women needed each other. My mother had to have a strong influence to prevent her from keeling over and Aunty Verma, well Aunty Verma being the kind of person she was needed to have someone to dominate and in mother she found a willing conquest.

After the first meeting, Rohit telephoned and said he would like to meet me again. We decided we would go out this time.

Aunty Verma got to hear of it the evening before and immediately flew over to our place. "We don't really know the boy, how can we allow Tara to go out with him alone?"

My mother protested, "It was the done thing now and a few meetings before deciding either way was not frowned upon like the old days. I trust Tara and have a sound feeling about Rohit, so its all right for them to go."

My mother's resolve was gradually worn down as always and she finally capitulated. It was decided that four of us would go out together so that Aunty Verma could "try and see him from our perspective and change her opinion about him" as she cleverly put it. I had never known her to change her opinion about anything and I knew it was just a ruse to go out for dinner.

As the clock ticked away, I got increasingly nervous. I was also in a bad mood. My hair always looked unruly as if I had just run my hands through it. It was cut short for purposes of convenience rather than an attempt to look attractive. Although I had good features the overall impression was one of ordinariness. I could have worked on myself but I never bothered. I was barely five feet tall and my diminutive size often had me overlooked even when I wasn't in a crowd.

I had made an attempt to have my hair done differently this time. It was cut short but longer on the sides as was the current fashion. My mother would have gone along with it but Aunty Verma got in before her. "Ahhugh! What have you done to yourself?" She was always such a good dramatist putting on a great act to go hand in glove with the words. Even though she was talking about my hair, she had to be at centre stage. Thus instead of everyone looking at my hair which was the cause of her exclamations and act, everyone was too busy looking at her because she was such a consummate actress.

Rohit was supposed to pick us up at eight-thirty since we didn't have a car. He was about ten minutes late because "of the traffic" but Aunty gave us a knowing looking straightaway. She sat in front with Rohit saying she got car sick at the back and there was nothing we could do except submit gracefully. However, I did not mind because there was a little song in my heart for Rohit had quietly told me I was looking very pretty.

On the way to the restaurant, Aunty having looked around the car, a Maruti 800, said, "there were so many of these on the roads these days one did not feel good about them any more. They were the common man's car. The car to have these days was the Maruti 1000, a Zen or Cielo." I fumed inwardly. The Cielo was barely on the roads and I thought she had a lot of nerve considering she did not even own a car! Rohit had adjusted his rear-view mirror and would periodically look at me intently, those moments had me mesmerised.

We eventually reached the restaurant and I heaved a sigh of relief. It was Chinese and was only a few weeks old.

But it had good reviews so we thought we would try it out. Under normal circumstances, it would have been too expensive for us.

It was dimly lit as was the norm but it had a pleasant feel about it and we sank into our seats with a sense of pleasure. Rohit was extremely attentive and I felt proud to be in his company. He managed to order even putting up with Aunty's fussiness and constant changing of dishes. She was in her element. "I would like some seaweed and made sure the chef doesn't burn it." There was no seaweed on the menu but Aunty got her way in the end, I thought the harassed waiter took pity on Rohit and himself!

Aunty had her nose up in the air that evening, all the dishes had something wrong with them and she insisted on eating with chopsticks. Rohit was really charming about the whole thing even when she dropped a piece of chicken coated in a black bean sauce on his stark white trousers.

I was too nervous to eat and played around with my food. Mother had never been a big eater and dinner was not her big meal of the day, so I cannot say she did it justice either. Rohit would probably have eaten a lot more but he was continually answering Aunty's questions and couldn't very well eat and talk together. The only person who did justice to the food was good old Aunty who helped herself to enormous portions all the while criticising the food.

The evening was a disaster as far as I was concerned and I was fuming inside. I thought Rohit would never want to see me again but as we got out of the car, Rohit quietly whispered if we could do it again and leave Aunty behind next time.

The next morning Aunty arrived just as I woke up and opened my eyes and pronounced the evening to be an indifferent one and no, she had not changed her opinion about Rohit one bit!

23

A newly-wed resplendent in a red and gold *paithani* sari joined our group and immediately became the centre of attention. "How long have you been married . . . ?" "Three weeks is nothing." "You plan to wear your *chura* for a year; how refreshing!" "Arranged marriage?" "But are you happy?

Looking at this blushing bride, I remember how it was when I was getting married.

That Rohit had wanted to marry her was more happiness than she could bear. Since his acceptance, Tara felt a joy unlike anything she had ever experienced. Any happiness for her had been momentary, very soon it had dissipated to be replaced by one of the baser emotions.

Now, her feelings were infinite. They stretched to every pore of her being and completely enslaved her with its buoyancy. She radiated happiness and her days were spent in fanciful dreams that lifted her spirits so that she was walking on air.

She was also petrified. She had finally found a man who was an embodiment of everything good. He was physically attractive as well as understanding. Who else would put up with Aunty Verma on a dinner date and not complain once or lose his temper? He spoke well and was charming to her mother. He had a good job as the manager of a huge multinational company and wanted to better himself. Most of all he was well-off and would take her out of the *mohalla* she longed to leave. What if it was just a dream and she woke up one morning to find, poof! There was nothing there. What then?

Those days her emotions see-sawed playing havoc with her equilibrium. She alternated between bouts of ecstasy and pangs of intense misery. It was unlike anything she had ever experienced.

Tara listened to Aunty Verma and her mother discussing the party or rather Aunty Verma was talking while my mother was allowed to make a comment once in a while.

When the news of Rohit's acceptanc arrived, my mother was unusually happy. "He said *yes*, he said *yes* she kept repeating softly with a wobbly smile on her face. It would have been too much to expect my mother to scream for joy or even laugh loudly showing her intense happiness. She was not used to good news and this particular news was too good to be true. Rohit's parents had talked to her directly so there was no about it was true. But the actual ceremony had not taken place. Till that happened she had to be cautious, had to hold herself back. That's the way my mother was. But it's not that she didn't show her happiness, she just showed it in a different way.

She pulls me aside and taking my comb from my hand tells me to sit on the ground. This is a ritual I love but is sparingly accorded to me. She starts humming under her breath and I let myself go limp against her body as she combs my hair with quick firm strokes, moving the hair from side to side to an unknown rhythm. After she had somewhat soothed my coarse hair into some semblance of discipl she would plait it tightly and neatly with a coloured ribbon and let it fall with some remnant of grace at the nape of my neck. I still relax against her despite her finished task revelling in the nearness that itself was so rare.

We had never had a very easy relationship, my mother

and I. We never showed our affection for each other through touching or holding. Physical demonstrations of any kind were not looked upon favourably in our house. I would watch my other friends share their affection, openly hugging and talking about their feelings. I often wondered why we never did the same. But we just never did. I think neither of us were very physical people and to change now would have proved embarrassing to both of us.

But after I got engaged there was a definite change in our relationship. We still did not touch each other or discuss our emotions but we became more conscious of each other. As if we realised the pattern of our life was changing and this was all the time we would have together. We both became more protective, more in sync, wishing to do everything for the other and often found ourselves enmeshed in emotions that we could not give voice to. It was a special time, when I no longer saw her as weak and diffident and she chose to forget I was a failure and was, for now, simply her cherished daughter.

Once the wedding date was decided, my mother wasted no time in sending out the news to all our relatives who quickly arrived in response to her summons. It was decided that the house was too small to accommodate the guests and relatives and plus it wasn't a very good address. A house was rented in a good locality, and the services of a cook and maid were arranged.

Two days after we moved the relative peace of the house seemed a thing of the past. The house took on a festive air amidst cries from every quarter. "Hurry up and have a bath, let other people use the bathroom." "Has anyone seen my pink sari?" "*Arrey ji,* someone has taken my sari!" "Where are the servants, it's lunch time and there is no food on the table?" "Help! Help! This stupid dog is following me. Help." And between this stir, preparations for the wedding continued.

A tailor was also hired to prepare the bridal trousseau and the many outfits that were part of the gift-giving ceremony. Throughut those days, you could hear the whirr of his sewing machine competing with the smell of the *halwai* and the abuse of the servants. Sometimes, one obliterated the other but it did not last for long as the other noise came back into the frey, with added vengeance to make up for their momentary absence.

Aunty Verma was bequeathed the title of Chairman which she enjoyed enormously despite the show of disdain and pretence at indifference. The house reverberated with noise. The chatter of different groups. Whispers at midnight and at dawn, loud shouts and back slapping in the morning, intense discussions and fevered arguments. The laughter that never quite died down despite the shushing and shooing at night. The made up songs that were in tune with the beat of the *dholak* and the graceful rhythm of impromptu dances. The tinkle of bangles and the vociferous clap of hands like thunder.

Relatives arrived from all over the country and immediately made themselves comfortable. All types of bedding and matresses were seen piled high in different rooms, items of clothing, both washed and unwashed were strewn all over the house, children played games and laughed and cried as they were wont to. The women were constantly huddled in groups discussing every little detail from jewellery, saris, flowers, *mithai* and money to be spent and gifts given. The men-folk gave their advice when asked but for the most part they sat in groups discussing some issue or the other, going for walks in the evening or escorting the women when needed. The acknowledged head of all this was none other than Aunty Verma. She was not staying at the house but was there every morning at the crack of dawn and left late in the evening after a full day spent dictating and bullying others.

Indian weddings are such busy affairs and there is so much to do that often the person whose wedding it is gets sidelined and spends a lot of time on her own as I did. But I welcomed the peace and solitude for I had a lot to think about, especially how I was going to manage my future.

When I got married my mother found it very difficult to contain her excitement. For the first time her daughter was coming out on top. This was a marriage that many in our locality would talk about for a long time and best of all it had stumped Aunty Verma. As the *doli* was leaving and we were walking towards the bridal car, Aunty Verma on one side and my mother on the other, she said loud enough for everyone to hear, "I always knew you could do it. Doesn't matter you didn't do well at cookery classes or painting. This is what you have excelled at" and with that she threw a triumphant look at Aunty who for once had nothing to say!

24

I learned to love Rohit dearly even though I had initially married him to escape from the suffocation that was threatening to engulf me in the form of Aunty Verma and the narrow confines of our locality.

Of course, there is always a little more than just that. I really married him for all the wrong reasons. To escape from the narrow-minded conserves of the *mohalla* I lived in. The idea of living in a better, more up-market part of the city filled me with excitement and I believed that all the stories about modern living would come true.

The first few days after our marriage I lost the bravado and felt sick with anxiety wondering when he was going to jump on top of me and claim his conjugal rights. When he was in the bedroom, I would feel goose pimples all over my body. But the first few days he was kindness itself and though we slept on the same bed, he did not initially touch me.

Presented with this kind of patience and understanding, I gave of myself completely when we finally consummated our marriage. The act itself is highly over rated. I found it messy and painful in the extreme. Rohit did not feel the same way for he took me thrice that first night and after that for months on and we would do it at least once every night.

I felt extremely nervous when Rohit took off my clothes. I was naked literally but inside me, I felt exposed and I did not like it at all. He was a gentle and considerate lover but I have to be honest and say that I did not enjoy myself. At best I suffered Rohit's caresses.

When he put his tongue in my mouth I found the sensation, while not exactly unpleasant, extremely invading. His finger on my breasts, stomach and vagina were not exactly welcome. I have never seen a grown man naked and Rohit's obvious hairiness dismayed me. When he thrust himself inside, it was painful. "It will be better next time, Tara," he murmured between kisses but it was always the same. I was always too dry and tight for him and thus I found our love making more of an ordeal than a pleasure.

I never let Rohit know how I felt. Later on, I learnt to appear physically involved while my mind was busy plotting new strategies to aid our rise up the corporate ladder. But that was later.

Tara divided women into two categories; those who were flowers and hence meant to be pampered and those who gave life to flowers, that is, made the decisions and were hence more in command – the gardener. A long time ago she decided that the best thing for her to be was the gardener even though in her heart she yearned to be a flower. It was a disastrous situation for her to be in. She had got herself immersed in a role that was not to her liking, that she had bought on upon herself and she ended up feeling resentful because she wanted to be cossetted by Rohit, instead of always being the person everyone depended on.

She saw her mother as a flower and look where it had got her. Practically, the whole neighbourhood dominated her. But she failed to see that the soil and environment had to be right to produce the right kind of seedling.

Although I never wanted to be like my mother, I learnt a lot from her that helped me in my new home. She taught me how to control my wild temper and appear sweetness itself, and never let on that the other party had got under your skin. She had perfected the art herself with Aunty

Verma and it was a kind of self-preservation mechanism that prepared her for the snide remarks and cruel barbs that came her way.

She also taught me never to reveal myself fully; "to do so is to put yourself in the other person's power. If you keep something back it can be used later, *that* is real power." She would reveal these simple truths in basic language not able to coat them in more powerful terms that might have given it more effect but the message was clear; knowledge is power and withheld secrets give one even more power.

It is difficult for two women to live together. Each needs her own space on which to paint the kind of canvas that matters to her. Inevitably, others involved get caught in the fray between the two and life often is as much hell for them as for those two. It is a kind of shuffle of power with one refusing to give up what she naturally sees as hers and the other is all intent on wrenching from her what she also naturally sees as the inevitable change of guard. Both sides are right but then the equanimity never really loses its hostility. Living within the same perimeters little darts of poison are shot out now and then. That was what life was like for me with my mother-in-law. Little darts of posion being shot around the house all day. Each round had its own victor and intially it was always her. But as the years went by, I started notching them under my belt. The balance was tilted very subtly.

It is difficult to explain but what really happens is this: You get married to a virtual stranger, you may meet and talk and sweeten your time together by donning a mantle that separates the real you from the artificial you and so, for all practical purposes you put on your best garb so you don't really see the negative in the other person. You get married and move to your new home which is your husband's but is not in a way. Because actually the people who really run the house are your in-laws and especially your mother-in-law. Since your husband has always been living according to her ways, he does not see any need for him to change. Things go on as usual without making any allowances for the new person, who breathes new life or tries to breathe new life into the old situation. Of course this is where the problem arises. The old guard resists change and that is the beginning of the end of the relationship unless of course if you can temper yours to suit her situation.

Eventually what happens is that the husband over the years becomes dependent on the wife more than the mother and slowly shifts allegiance and then the fireworks start! This is a foregone scenario but once in a while someone like Tara comes along and upsets the cartwheel.

My mother-in-law and I did not exactly see eye to eye when I entered my new home. Among other things, she had an annoying habit of standing by my side when I was cooking in the kitchen. She would not say a word but each time I put in an ingredient she did not think I needed or I was too liberal with the oil, she would purse her lips together and a loud snort-like noise like "hummmph" would escape from either her nose or her lips. I was never really sure despite making a definite attempt to find out. At first, I would be nervous and unsure, dropping the bottle of spices or putting too much of this and too little of that. Finally, I plucked up enough courage and told her I couldn't cook properly with her standing over me. She took great exception to that remark and for days she went around with a swollen face. She refused to talk to me directly and whenever we were both in the kitchen she would talk loudly to the servants and make loud noises with the pots and pans. A loud "hummmph" frequently escaped from her.

The situation continued for many days and the impasse

seemed unbridgeable. The banging and the "hummmphing" went on for a few days getting worse all the time before I took the situation in hand by placating the old lady and asking for her advice on the *Hyderabadi biryani* which I publicly acknowledged at the dinner table no one could make better than her. This so-called giving in was part of my mother's advice: "Better to retreat tactically and save face rather than burn the bridge which will link you to your house."

I see my mother-in-law now as nothing more than a frightened old woman who was lost in waters that were proving too powerful for her. She was trying to be friends, to form some kind of bond without appearing to give in to anything. But what is true is that even your own mother irritates you at times and with all the fears and pre-conditioning with which one enters a new house, it is difficult to completely accept a mother-in-law unless both sides compromise.

Tara's mother-in-law was undergoing similar fears. She was apprehensive and unsure about the changes that had taken place in her household. Where was her place in it? Did she even have a place? Her mother-in-law had treated her in the same manner and she was perpetuating the same crime not because she was a bad person but because she knew no better. Otherwise, who would protect her? She had struggled to build a position for herself in the household and now some upstart was going to take it away from her?

After this fracas, I decided the time had come to face the problem head-on. I looked for her all over the house but she seemed to have disappeared. The fire had been there, I had not imagined it but now like a wisp of smoke, it was gone.

I went to her bedroom to look for her. The room was surrounded on all sides by enormous expanses of glass which provided breathtaking views. At that moment, the sun is waylaid outside and filters through at the occupants desire through bamboo-blinds. The white muslin curtains offer a great relief of coolness as do the bare brown floors that are instantly healing. The huge palms and ficus plants are all part of the effect. It is not unlike an oasis in the desert only more real than imaginary.

I looked at her photographs; smiling into some unknown lensmen's eyes, looking romantically at her husband, holding her son up high. They were loving photographs, they showed a picture of a woman I had never seen. Why, why did she dislike me so?

I heard a soft sound from her dressing-room and looked in. She was fast asleep on her pink *chaise-lounge*. She looked like the younger version I had just seen in the photographs. She was snoring softly, her mouth was slightly open and the strong lines that ran from her nostrils to her mouth were gone. The fight seemed to have gone out of her and she looked frail and defenceless. Her legs were curled up and both her hands were tucked under her chin in the foetal position.

I felt bad about the fight earlier and my rudeness towards her. In the heat of the moment, I had wished her dead and I felt a shiver of remorse sweep over me as I looked upon her sleeping form. As I stood looking at her and lost in my own thoughts, she must have woken up. But she did not get up, she just looked at me till the penetration of her stare must have broken through my reverie.

We just stared at each other for what must have been a few seconds but seemed like a long, long moment. Nobody said anything. I certainly did not know what to say. After the horrible fight to be found in her bedroom which I rarely ventured into and caught watching her sleeping was disquieting. But because of that transgression, I had seen another side of her and my emotions seesawed from intense burning anger for what I saw as her delight in making me feel like an outsider to a glimpse of her vulnerability that brought her down from the position of ogre to that of a mere woman, frightened by the changes in her household and holding on because she didn't know what else to do.

She got up in a fluster, patting her hair and pulling her fallen *pallu* into place, in obvious embarrassment. "Is something the matter?" she asked and even her face lines didn't seem as harsh and there was a note of genuine worry in her voice.

"No . . . no, nothing's wrong. I . . . I just wanted to see . . . see if you were all right. I heard a sound and . . . came here." I was nervous and flustered and unsure of what I should or should not say.

"Well, that's good," she said dryly. "So if it's fine with you I will just go back to sleep."

It was not a real question, of course. She had dismissed me as if I was a child and there was nothing I could do but retreat quickly. As I stumbled out of the room, I happened to glance back unconsciously. She was watching me closely. There was gentle look on her face and the lines had almost disappeared.

She covered her back well and there seemed to be no hidden chink in her armour. But the incident in her bedroom sowed the seeds of a connection, albeit a fragile one and things soon changed.

I realised that I had finally seen through those barriers and penetrated the sham she had erected around hereself. She was an old woman who used indifference as a cloak, anger as a shield and silence as a weapon to combat the enemy, the threatening outsider. Times would teach her that these weapons were useless for the enemy was lurking somewhere else; deep within her.

25

Discontent played a big part in Tara's upbringing. She was always having to do without and the material hardship had embittered her. She had occasionally wallowed in self-pity and complained bitterly to her mother selfishly attacking her for their impecunious state. But by and large, she had known none of the above were going to help her. Now married and appreciably better off, she was determined to change things. She was no longer willing to accept the same kind of drudgery and painful anonymity.

Having spent her life in passive acceptance of what fate had in store for her and completely overshadowed by Aunty Verma and her daughter, she looked forward to marriage. Marriage would bring a definite freedom from those two, while an idyllic existence would see expectations fulfilled.

Tara had come to the house as a young bride whose smooth baby-faced features belied the strength of purpose and determination that existed in her small frame. Very early in her life, she decided she did not want to be like her mother; vague and constantly overlooked. She wanted to be the pivot around which everyone else moved. Thus, with a degree of ruthlessness and keeping this constant in her mind she set about her task. She worked slowly and methodically and little by little, imperceptibly she made the house and its inhabitants revolve around her.

Her mother-in-law who was initially on her guard, grew to depend on her. No task was too mundane, no request ever denied. She took her out shopping, dropped her at lunch parties, her card sessions, took her to the beauty parlour and run whatever small errands she needed. She went for walks with her father-in-law, read the newspaper and magazines with him, listened to his at times boring monologues about his cronies.

She threw herself into the act with great abandon and any self-questioning was ruthlessly put aside. She became the perfect homemaker, the complete hostess. A hopeless cook, she became a chef *par excellence*, serving mouth-watering dishes that complemented each person's taste. *Idlis, dosas, paranthas* and *cholas* were her father-in-law's breakfast, while cereal with *croissants* were her mother-in-law's morning repast.

There was a single-mindedness that prevented her from deviating from her chosen path. The years of living on the fringe with her mother had made her determined to have a different life. She learnt how to make vegetables last longer, the cream from the milk was religiously collected and any loose change was zealously coveted. Thus trouser pockets were always turned inside out and tips were kept to a minimum. She would haggle for hours over prices and walked farther in the market to get the best produce.

Tara saved her money in an old tea-tin. Every week, she would take the money out and count the crisp notes and loose change closing her eyes and breathing in the fragant smell of orange and cinammon that had attached itself to the secret hoard. The weekly exercise and the secrecy attached gave her an almost sensual thrill that was never matched by Rohit's lovemaking.

She never gave the impression of being stingy. Guests were generally overwhelmed with her hospitality, only she knew the lengths she had to go to keep it that way.

She hated being a nobody, disliked being overlooked and decided early on that through her husband's career, his clients and associates, she was going to be somebody. She acquainted herself with her husband's business and managed to talk intelligently with his company executives without appearing too intelligent, or she knew she would frighten them away. She knew when to ask the right questions without appearing too much of a brain and could flatter a man with the right words. She practised her laughter so it would not appear too girlish, too sure of herself and even too affected. Just the right combination at the right time to soothe a man's ego. However, for the ladies she put on a different front. She appeared friendly and interested but slightly unsure and at times even naïve when it suited her purpose. After all, who knew better than she about the intricate machinations a woman was prey to?

Tara was determined to "get with" the right set. And if that meant doing the done thing then so be it. One of the so-called "done things" was riding. Tara had no particular liking for any animal and horses in particular frightened her. She was scared of falling off them while riding. And yet she endured the agonising rides and bruising aftermath and managed to give the appearance of enjoyment all because it was "the done thing!" She even learnt to play golf. It bored her immensely but it was the best way to meet more business people, be in the right *milieu*. She became so adept at playing her part that when new people joined the group, she could feign with great authority, "Don't tell me! You must be joking! You don't have a horse, you don't play golf?" When someone timidly enquired if she did, she answered vigorously: "Of course I ride and play golf. What a question! I've been doing both as far back as I can remember!"

She gave generously to all causes where her name was prominently displayed though it hurt her to part with the money but she knew it was the right thing to do. She was living her life not the way she wanted to but the way she thought she was supposed to. It was a grin-and-bear situation in which she never really let her inhibitions down. So that although people never caught on she always appeared somewhat strained and false.

She tried to emulate high society ladies by watching carefully and practising in the privacy of her bedroom. She learnt that being direct and straightforward never paid nor did committing oneself because then you could never be pinned down to anything. There were ways of saying things and soon she mastered the art of double speak. When an interfering though influential busy body made a nuisance of herself instead of being blunt and telling her to mind her own business, a more suitable way of putting it would be to say: "How kind of you to think of me but please do not worry yourself about me." It was far better than saying, "mind your own business!"

Tara was an enigma. Racked by insecurities, she nevertheless managed to mask her many deep-rooted fears and presented the world with an alternate picture which she had strived hard to achieve. Her insatiable appetite for glamour infused the ordinary and mundane with great passion and took it out of its narrow confines to give it luminosity and depth.

She had become quite the society lady. Among her group, she set the trends and decided what was in fashion and what had become passe. She enjoyed the position, after all she had worked hard for it. It gave her a thrill when the younger ladies came to ask her for advice and tried to emulate her. It was a far cry from her mother's small one bedroom flat.

Rohit went along with her. She could be very persuasive when she wanted and he was not averse to going higher up the corporate ladder. But his attempts were at best mediocre and without her relentless moves the act would have ended with a whimper. He did not, however, see behind the scenes to know the great effort that was put into every move. The friendships that were to be cultivated, the right word to the boss' wife. She gave wonderful little dinner parties; throwing the right crowd together, the latest band was always playing, the food was superb and the drinks were the best in town. She had got Rohit to perfect the art of cocktails such as Boilermaker, a whisky and beer concoction or a white rum, blue curacaco and coconut drink called Blue Hawaiian. Other cocktails like Virgin's Prayer and Slow Comfortable Screw were popular more for their names and the titters they produced than the actual contents. Rohit's cocktails were in great demand by ladies who did not drink alcohol for he improvised excessively and produced with great fanfare Peach, Apple and Ginger slings, mango-based Caribbean Cocktails and even the ubiquitous Iced Mint-Tea had good innings in the sweltering summer heat.

The move up the corporate ladder came swiftly. They changed house three times before they settled into the present one which had five bedrooms and an exquisite garden to go with it. There were three indoor servants, a gardener and two drivers.

Tara reigned like a queen. Her home was run like a well-oiled machine and she was at the centre of that hub. No decision was taken without her and she often acted for all of them, Rohit having submerged his will to hers in deference to its perspicacity. She was now somebody in society. Her husband was doing well, she had a fabulous house and gave wonderful parties. She had many friends who were always asking her advice and was on several committees. She had succeeded by sheer perseverance and hard work.

If there were any doubts she quelled them, pushing them aside and squashing them into pulp before they could germinate. At times if she seemed unhappy, she could not really pinpoint why. She never allowed herself to reach the point of questioning because there could be no turning back. The die had been cast a long time ago and the bridge back was only a shadowy remnant of another time. But still she felt an ache within her, of something lost, some precious past destroyed. She did not give into this soul searching, it was useless to get into the whys and the hows, rather she obliterated it ruthlessly and believed it could not, would not take root again.

26

I was shaken out of my reverie by the commotion that was Aunty Verma greeting her daughter Mala who had arrived earlier from America. Once again I saw Aunty Verma's acting talent on display. Most people at the party turned to look at the noise generated by the old lady leaving Aunty Verma smug and satisfied.

Aunty Verma was tactless and thick-skinned, a dangerous combination for the recipient of her sharp tongue. There was not an ounce of femininity about her and this was highlighted by an aggressiveness that almost always put people on their guard. Invariably, Aunty Verma would pounce on women with more feminine attributes and men of a more docile nature were not left undisturbed.

She had an uncanny sense of timing and was a great actress. Thus she could weave a dramatic moment from nothing and have us all spellbound in its clutches even though the attention should really be on something or someone else. I found her irritating and exasperating and there were times when I would gladly have throttled her. But despite her often infuriating behaviour, she was a part of my childhood and I tolerated her. I could not say the same for her daughter.

Mala was back in town. For months, we had been hearing of her impending visit from Aunty Verma and now she was here. Mother wanted me to go to the airport but I declined. I could already feel the same insecurities rising within me and that sense of dread that always dogged me when these two were around.

The entire *mohalla* had come out to see her when she arrived in the taxi, Aunty Verma had wanted to borrow one of the cars but I had refused saying Rohit needed them both that day. It was a lie of course, I could use the car any time but I was giving in to some inner memories that guided my action and which I did not subdue.

Everyone was standing outside her flat and ours with huge smiles on their faces and one or two of the neighbours were even holding garlands. I could see my mother with them, she had of course gone to the airport. I watched as Mala got out of the taxi with a huge smile on her face. She had put on weight, you could see that at once. She was wearing a pair of jeans that seemed too small for her and a printed shirt with huge flowers on it. Her hair was short and curly and made her face seem much rounder than it actually was. She was wearing high heels which I thought showed her lack of taste.

They were down there for almost ten minutes before Aunty Verma decided enough was enough and beckoned her daughter inside. I knew I should go and see her straightaway before it was to late and mother started asking questions. But my feet seemed to be made of clay and my body refused to respond to commands from my brain.

My mother came looking for me as I knew she would. She was frowning heavily. "What is wrong with you, Tara? Your oldest friend is here and you haven't been to meet her?"

"She is not my oldest friend, mama. How many times have I told you that? And I was just coming, what's the hurry anyway?" I muttered angrily.

My mother did not like that one bit and started one of her long sermons. I thought it better to go and see Mala than listen to her and I hastily escaped.

She was nice to me, apologising for not being able to attend my wedding and thanking me for the lovely photographs I had sent. I was about to protest but realised mother must have sent them on my behalf. We talked about general issues, there were several other neighbours around and she was constantly fielding their questions. When I got up to leave, I felt a great sense of relief and chided myself for my stupidity. We were both married women now, she was hardly likely to say anything nasty and especially when she had got all she had aspired for.

Two days later my mother invited Rohit and myself for dinner. She didn't mention anyone else joining us so it was a shock to find Mala and Aunty Verma along with my cousin *masi* and *masar*. I looked at my mother accusingly but she refused to meet my eyes. So, there we were having dinner like the old times.

My mother was an excellent cook, today she had excelled herself. The meat *biryani* was delicious and authentically *dhumed* in the *Hyderabadi* style. The rice grains were separate as they should be and the *ghosht* was succulent and tender. The *kakori kebab* was softness itself and melted in the mouth with each bite. The garlic *dahi* was creamy and like everything else was in plentiful supply.

Everyone ate with their fingers, prodding them to move faster and faster to keep pace with their greedy stomachs that heaved with satisfaction as another morsel found its way down. For a time there was a lull in the conversation as we all concentrated on the food and treated it with the reverence it deserved.

Dessert was home-made *kulfi* replete with *badaams* and *falooda*. Although everyone was full they could not refuse, knowing it would be the best *kulfi* they would have in a long time. Tara took a spoonful of *kulfi* and relaxed.

Dinner was almost over and nothing upsetting had happened so far. I was feeling light-headed and listening to the conversation around me.

Rohit was talking to my mother about his parents and my father-in-law's *penchant* for reading. "…Yes, it's amazing the speed with which he goes through a book."

Aunty Verma was in her element and was talking knowledgeably about America to my mother's cousin, though she had not to my knowledge made a trip there yet. But she had an avid listener in Geeta *Masi* who sat listening to her with a glazed look on her face. "The best place to get bargains and real value for money is the factory outlets. You can find items for less than half the price you would pay otherwise. Look at Mala's dress," a bright multi-coloured piece that was ghastly and looked like a reject from Janpath than something she had bought from America.

My *Masar*, a quiet man who hardly ever said anything, told me in his squeaky voice I was looking much better after my marriage. "I think it has a lot to do with your new hair style."

I had grown it long despite its heaviness and had it straightened regularly. It was the new look and coupled with a centre parting it helped me appear calm and poised. I turned to smile at him and thank him for his kind words and saw Mala had also heard his words.

"Yes, you have changed a lot since I last saw you," she said from the other corner of the table. I had deliberately chosen to sit away from her.

The rest of the conversation around us stopped as the focus shifted to both of us.

I did not want to get into anything controversial so I smiled and said as casually as I possibly could, "everyone changes after marriage." It was a non-committal remark and I hoped she would drop the conversation.

But she did not.

"That's true but you've changed quite dramatically," she said, arching one of her eyebrows in a manner I had come to dread.

"Quite dramatically."

I could feel my heart beating faster: *dhum, dhum, dhum.* There was a rush in my ears, my face was becoming hot and flushed and I was starting to twist my hands, something I did when I got nervous. I could sense the danger but I knew I could not retreat. I had no alternative but to say limply, "How do you mean, dramatically?"

"Well you were a little mouse when I left and now you are quite the lady." Before I could recover from that snide remark, she went for my hair. "And where does this transformation take place? At Express Yourself or from Hair Delight's?"

Express yourself was the best salon in town, terribly expensive and catered to the city's elite, while Hair Delight's was our own neighbourhood hairdresser who cut both men and women's hair.

"This transformation," I replied a trifle shortly, "is done by Mr Raju." She knew my hair well, it was curly and bushy and I always had it in a short style because otherwise it was unmanageable.

She lifted both eyebrows now, looking like something out of a Hindi horror movie and feigning disbelief said, "you mean he's still around?"

"Of course, why wouldn't he be?" The words tumbled out before I could stop them.

"Well, I heard he had this terrible skin disease and that it was contagious. It is called something …dem …dermititis and flares up occasionally becoming all gooey and pusy.

Where had she heard this living in America while I living in close proximity to the man had never heard anything of the sort? I felt miserable and my sense of calm totally deflated.

She gushed, "I have this wonderful guy in the States called Carl who does my hair. He's so cute and understands my hair wonderfully. You know the texture, the length, the roots. Americans are such great people, they go into the whole thing and understand it fully before deciding what looks good on you."

I looked at her across the table and felt like throttling her. Why, why when I was settling down did she have to come back? I felt like a little girl again, always losing to her. I bit my lip to stop it from trembling.

As if at a distance I heard a voice, a squeaky voice cut across the conversation. "I still think Tara looks much better after her marriage."

27

I felt a sharp nudge on my midriff that shook me out of my miserable reverie and looked to see the lady next to me soundlessly urging me to look at Sheila who had drunk too much and was making eyes at a younger man while her husband was trying hard to contain his jealousy.

Jealousy was an emotion I had grown up with. It attached itself to me like a leech and drew out my baser emotions with skill and precision. But still it did not prepare me for the searing heat that burned through me when I found Rohit was having an affair. This type of jealousy was more overpowering and refused to be calmed, it lashed within me like a tidal wave and grew to yeast-sized proportions consuming me from within. It stuck to my skin so that I could hardly breathe and frayed my nerves like red hot chillies. The rage I felt was raw and alive, it burned within me and contaminated my senses.

At that moment, Rohit appeared by my side and gesturing towards my empty glass asked if I wanted a refill. I gladly acquiesed and followed him to the bar.

He was so tender and loving, looking after my every need but I still could not blot out the terrible time I went through when I found he was having an affair. I thought I had my life, and that included my husband, under control.

Rohit was an easy going sort of fellow in many ways

but when his mind was made up about something there was nothing that could make him change his mind for he stuck to his guns like his life depended upon it.

And his mind was made up about his wife. He found her ruthless and completely single-minded. The characteristics he had grown to admire were now too overpowering to live with. There was no longer any femininity and gentleness to Tara. He was going through that phase in his life when he felt he needed more excitement. He found that excitement in Dina. She was all that his wife was not. He had seen Tara change from a shy and diffdent young woman to a strong ambitious lady who pursued her goal with a relentlessness that left very little room for anything else. Tara did not realise it but she was fast becoming another Aunty Verma.

When Tara found out about Rohit's infidelity everything came to a standstill. All her dreams, her conniving, her persistent efforts – everything stopped. It was a profound betrayal, the years of sacrifice, the relentless pursuit of her dream was torn apart and contemptuously tossed aside.

At first she felt an acute sense of loss. But it was soon replaced by anger. Seething, scalding, lava like anger. After years of painstaking sacrifice, of iron self-control, of giving into others, this is what she got in return. How dare he destroy what she had worked so hard for? He had wanted it too, didn't he? *Or did he?*

After anger came the self-doubts and the questions to which she had to find the answers. Why? Why did he go to another woman, what did she lack that pushed him into someone else's arms?

With her inbuilt resilience that had weathered all kinds of storms, she looked for the answer for what she saw as a gross miscarriage of justice. And after much soul searching, she found the answer with in herself. She saw with blinding clarity that she was to blame. Her own need for recognition and the path towards that recognition had blinded her to Rohit's needs. What she had seen as wholehearted compliance was merely a brief acquiescence on his part, a giving in to her wishes because he loved her. But that compliance had long since disappeared. She had stopped asking and simply did as she pleased. That is when the link had been severed.

She knew she had to win Rohit back. The years of plotting and planning stood her in good stead. First, she decided she had to size up the opposition.

Dina Dixit looked like a cherubic nymph with her rotund body and trembling thighs Despite the extra layers everywhere, she exuded a voluptuousness that had men panting. Women who made the mistake of dismissing her as fat regretted their rejection of her physical attributes when they found their husbands following her like love-lorn puppies.

She was also the biggest movie star with a massive fan following that let her dictate the terms and amount of money she wanted.

At first I was intimidated by her. She was young and immensely confident and had her life ahead of her. When I looked at her, I felt a terrible sadness, as if everything, life itself had nothing enchanting in store for me. With my husband in her clutches, I had nothing left to look forward to. It would have been different if I was ten years younger but I no longer had it in me to compete with her. With a twist in my heart, I realised the battle was over before it had even started. She had him and there was nothing I could do about it.

Or was there?

Tara felt claustrophobic inside the room. People were everywhere and she could not breathe. She went to the garden.

The scene that presented itself before her eyes was breathtaking. The rhododendrons were lush, and magnificent in colouring while the azaleas had an exotic intensity difficult to miss. The nasturtiums were ablaze and were a sudden though pleasing contrast with the pale lilies. The trees were magnificent in their lushness providing a perfect backdrop to the plants.

She had sized Dina up correctly. She confronted her directly at a party and playing the nondescript mousy wife to a tee she begged for her husband back. It was a good move. Dina would have fought tooth and nail if she had been presented with a woman of the world. As it was this pathetic creature could have her husband back. Anyway she had only used Rohit to make her current beau jealous. He could now be dropped.

She remembered the conversation as if it was yesterday. The encounter had seared itself in her mind.

"I know this doesn't mean anything to you but I happen to love my husband very much and I also know he means nothing to you except a one night stand, a little distraction before someone or something better comes along."

She simply raised her eyebrows more arrogantly than ever, puffed on her cigarette and blew the smoke in my face. After what seemed an eternity of sitting like a frigid icicle, she observed: "You are a typically frightened housewife who is fast losing her husband and mind you," she said wagging her index finger at me, "mind you, not because of me but because you yourself are not keeping up with the times. Today, a man wants more than a mother look alike be it a younger one, today a man wants excitement and someone who can keep him interested. You have to move with the times and not remain stuck in a groove the way you have. You are right," she said taking a swig of her drink, "you are right when you say he means nothing to me. I'm just having a good time but if you want him so badly, I suggest you do something about it instead of going around giving speeches and looking like a frightened mouse."

She then just sat down on the swing and coolly sipped her drink. Tara didn't move for a long time. She stood in the corner just gazing out of the verandah without really seeing anything. It was obvious she was distraught and buried her head in her hands with obvious anguish.

My friends, Arundhati and Mina, were both standing there awkwardly. No one really ventured to say anything as the silence grew. Everyone was immaculately casual. Arundhati's face was expressionless while she toyed with her drink. Rohit moved towards the balcony and peered up and down as if he had found something very unusual. Tara wandered up and down the balcony while Dina sat in one of the cosy chairs and put her feet up as if she hadn't a care in the world and no intention whatsoever to move.

The conversation, the part that was reaching me as if from far away, seemed light and inconsequential. I tried valiantly several times to appear undisturbed.

To cut a long story short, the outcome of this *tete-a-tete* was quite surprising. Everyone thought Dina would continue to play her little vamp bit while Tara watched from the sidelines and Rohit would of course be totally impervious to everything but her. What happened was really quite extraordinary. Dina studiously avoided Rohit who was initially upset but then angrily kept away from her while Tara seemed to have acquired new strength and before our very eyes a metamorphosis gradually took place.

Tara changed her style of dressing, nothing drastic but

more than enough to make everyone sit up and notice. The sari was still there but it was now designer wear in bold colours. No longer was the *pallu* draped right across the shoulder, but was left hanging to the floor while the blouse had become a skimpy little number that revealed an attractive bare back and svelte midriff. The hair was no longer tied up or clumped in a bun but left flowing after successful trips to the beauty parlour and her make-up was applied ever so skilfully to make that all important difference. Eyebrows were arched and lashes were darker, the lids faintly shadowed and eyes made bigger with kohl. Her skin was immaculately made up with a rosy sheen and her lips were beautifully outlined. More people noticed her and parties were no longer as much agony as they used to be. She was slowly coming into her own and as was bound to happen one day when Rohit in a rare moment away from his customary self-absorption happened to look up, and what did he see . . . his attractive new wife, dazzling in appearance and soft and feminine as he wished her to be. Well, it was a new beginning!

It all seemed like a fairy tale but the truth was Dina had been struck by Tara's courage. She knew Tara did not have a chance when pitted against her and yet she had fought to save her marriage, because it was important to her. Dina admired that trait in her and despite her *filmi* reputation had no desire to break up a marriage. So, she had in fact had a helping hand in transforming her. Surprisingly, that was the beginning of a wonderful though incongruous friendship.

28

I went through a period of great uncertainty and anguish. My moods would constantly swing from despair to ecstasy depending on how I viewed the situation at that particular moment. Sometimes I would rage at the man, my anger brimming over when I remembered Dina and him together. But at other times, in more reflective moments, I wondered if I had not pushed him into her arms. And after all the most important point to remember was that he loved me. He would never stray again.

The first time he really noticed my changed mode of appearance I was wearing a skimpy halter top made of mirror work that really covered very little. My sari was gossamer chiffon and extremely flattering. My hair was pulled back high while my make up was heavier than usual and definitely more dramatic.

I deliberately arrived late at the party and walked in while not defiantly, with an exaggerated swagger. People turned round to stare, others whispered, while someone even whistled. Rohit noticed me then. I had to force myself to walk on as if I hadn't a care in the world. I could barely breathe and felt my palms go sweaty with the tension. But I refused to stop now.

I eventually managed to reach Tara and Arundhati and then I coolly looked back at my husband.

His face! The stunned look was more than I had hoped for. It was slowly replaced by a kind of dawning realisation of all that had happened between us. But I saw the love on his face. There was no doubt it was there.

Rohit gently took my hand and held on to it for dear

life. We were both highly emotional but did not say anything knowing we would have plenty if time for that later.

"Let me stop here now, dear reader. If I go on any further, I will start crying and I will not be able to tell you the rest of my story."

Rohit came and asked Tara if he could get her anything. Her glass was half full and she shook her head but he did not move away and instead he sat down beside her amidst a group of gaggling housewives.

He could see the men out of the corner of his eye whisper something and then laugh loudly, no doubt they were talking about him. But he didn't care. He wanted to be with Tara and look after her. He was her husband after all. He knew he was behaving out of character. Not many couples stayed together at parties. He watched Dina come in surrounded by a bevy of admirers. He had almost lost Tara because of his foolishness and it had frightened him as nothing before. It had shaken him out of his complacency. Now sitting beside his attractive wife, he realised he was the one who was unsure of her. Her new attractiveness scared him. What if she left him for someone else?

Usually it was Tara who felt insecure but her new found confidence made me feel unsure of myself and ambivalent about her feelings towards me.

I kept telling myself, reassuring myself actually, that she would never leave me. But I was not at all sure. This new Tara was someone very different from the woman I had married. She was poised and charming. She was incredibly attractive and I could see all the attention that came her way. She seemed oblivious to them all. I knew I was working myself into a panic thinking about all my insecurities. But for the first time in our married life the tables were reversed. We quarelled a few times then made up only to quarrel later. The more afraid I became of losing her the more possessive I became. Whenever she talked for too long to anyone, I found myself at her elbow and I could see she was irritated by this behaviour. I became short-tempered and began drinking more than I was used to. This inevitably made matters worse. I was going crazy and didn't know what to do about it.

How could I have been so blind? So ungrateful? Not to realise that what I had was a diamond. It needed polishing and I could have helped with that but instead, I had not seen its worth and had dumped it thinking it would always be there when I wanted it. She had endured my infidelity with great fortitude, while I, callous beast that I am, returned love and loyalty by showing up my contemptible weakness repeatedly.

But then I remembered Tara's talk on the balcony and her subsequent fight for me. Oh yes. There was no doubt that she had fought for me, for our marriage. Sure, she had changed in the process, but just knowing she loved me so much made me feel good. It gave me strength. I thereafter resolved to make my wife proud of me and work towards making my marriage a success.

29

Tara's mother-in-law, Mrs Kapur, was pleased to see Tara and Rohit sitting together so companionably. She had seen the strain on both of them and was glad her daughter-in-law had persevered to keep the marriage going.

I like my daughter-in-law. She is quiet and even cool but that is because she is constantly on her guard hoping no one will say anything to hurt her. And yet she has great, almost steel like resolve and determination that is unmatched. She does not know it but she is very much like me. Perhaps that is why I have been so distant towards her. It is not that I do not like her, I am just afraid of being trampled over and pushed into one corner. Nowadays young people are very selfish, you give them a little, they want all of it. She thinks I don't like her but I need more time. I cannot just accept her new ways immediately, the thirty years I have lived here cannot be swept under the carpet in a day. I will let go, but slowly, I hope she has the patience to wait.

I know what it is like to be young and unsure, to dream, to want, to yearn, only to find fate has dealt you some other hand.

Kishore Malhotra, a regular party drunk, was holding court at the centre of the room.

He beat his wife regularly and everyone knew it. There was no point concealing it anyway. Not when she could be seen at various parties sporting different bruises each time.

At first she had tried to hide it and so did he, feigning nonchalance and total surprise. But now neither of them bothered with the pretence. She was resigned while he railed at womankind in particular and everyone in general.

"Women need to be beaten now and then to remind them of their place. Look at my wife, she knows who the boss is and never dares cross the limits." It was the kind of cliched talk that an insensitive man made to other insensitive men.

Most people did not like him but what kept him on everyone's social list was the fact that he was rich and I mean *really* rich. And he could get things done. If someone needed to bump someone off he could take care of it, if a guy had to be beaten up then Kishore was the man to turn to. He could take care of all kinds of inconveniences for you and he never seemed to ask for anything in return. But he was there at the top of everyone's party list. It was a small price to pay.

Tara had not been able to meet Mina or Arundhati yet. Each time she tried to cross the labryinthine space of the room she was cut of by some acquaintance or the other. There was plenty of social liasing. "Hello dear, so nice to see you again..." "What a gorgeous sari – you always look so good." "Tara my dear, you look divine!" "I must tell you what happened the other day..." At other times, the two were busy. It was expected of Mina, she was so gregarious but today even the normally reserved Arundhati was being kept busy.

Tara loved both Arundhati and Mina and wished she could be a little like both of them. She had observed them thoroughly and come to the conclusion that while Arundhati was naturally the more regal, it was Mina who had more friends. Each had characteristics that she wished she possessed. On the one hand, she wanted to have Arundhati's regal bearing and the impeccable style that went with it but if one is aloof and distant, she often mused then it is impossible to have the affection of people, as Mina so obviously did.

Mina was genuinely popular with most people. They were attracted to her smiling face, her real concern and her ability to make everyone seem special. She had a self-possession about her that attracted those who were unsure and an easy going manner that signalled a friend to the confident. At a party it was always Mina who managed to break through one's reserve and the friendships that were formed carried on because others persevered out of genuine affection for her.

True, both Arundhati and she had people swarming around them at parties, but she knew that in Arundhati's case it was because of who she was; the royal as well as monetary power proved irresistible to most people. In her case, she had to work hard to cultivate the right kind of friends. And she was sure that the falseness and shallow charm could never take the place of genuine warmth.

After much concentrated observation, Tara eventually came to understand the essence that was Mina. Mina was genuinely interested in everything and everyone around here. It was not an act. How else could one define the look of interest and the twinkle in her eyes as she talked to someone? The small gestures that were neither cloying nor affected but were naturally soothing and complemented the soft voice that was replete with inflection. She spoke well and her command of the language was perfect. She knew the appropriate word and conveyed it at the right moment. There were no barriers surrounding her, rather a warm acceptance of everyone she took to her heart without reservation. Her magic was elusive and could not be emulated and Tara could only watch in admiration this wonderful cherished friend in action.

Tara also loved the way Arundhati did everything. She was the opposite of herself. Graceful and dignified, whether it was ordering the servants, presiding over a boring dinner party or talking to her son – she always did everything with style. She, on the other hand, felt all the more brash and overbearing in front of her delicate persona. But Arundhati never made her feel that way deliberately. It was just the way she was. Tara admired her and tried to emulate her refined manner and dignified presence.

30

I remembered the first time I had been privy to Arundhati's confidence. She told me all about Avinash and her married life, her expectations and her dreams. She also told me about the disillusionment, the anger and eventual acceptance.

After she spoke there was silence. I was stunned for a moment. I had not expected such honesty, such forthrightness and for a moment I was caught off balance groping for the right words to show I understood her private pain.

I could see her relax as I spoke. I saw that she had almost regretted her impulse to speak but she was letting go slowly as I spoke. I tried hard, there was no way I was going to rebuff someone who had the guts to speak from her heart. Something extremely rare in our society.

The words came tumbling out. There was no restraint and I provided none. I just listened as her words became more and more vibrant infused with a passion that was otherwise stifled. It was remarkable that such a woman could go through life denying herself, her very persona and appearing just as others wanted her to be and not as she was.

I put my head on Rohit's shoulder and silently thanked God for giving me a second chance. Although Arundhati was glad we had patched up our marriage and I was giving Rohit another chance, Mina did not approve. She believed I was capable enough to start on my own.

"Why do you need a man who has cheated on you and

since he has done it before the likelihood of his straying again is almost predictable," she had said angrily.

"I love him, Mina. Isn't that a good enough reason?"

"Not when you lose your self-respect," she retorted sharply.

"Love is a beautiful word that covers a multitude of emotions. It stands for all that is right and the good that develops between people. But when it clouds your mind and becomes a negative emotion then 'love' on its own has no meaning."

"Don't you believe in giving a person a second chance, isn't that the right thing to do? After all," Tara continued heatedly, "people do change and one has to put one's faith somewhere?"

Mina caught hold of her hand and said gently, "Tara I do believe in second chances. You know what a mockery of a marriage I have and oh, how I would love to get a second chance. But all I am saying is stand up for yourself, so that others can look up to you and respect you. Without respect the marriage is doomed. Nobody should be able to take you for granted or play with your emotions the way Rohit has."

But I knew Rohit was not completely at fault. The blame also lay with me. But apart from that I am a practical woman and realised that without Rohit, I would never amount to anything. The home, the lifestyle, my very status, were linked to my marriage with him. Take them away and I was back to being the old Tara I had left behind in my mother's house. Anyhow what was the point of being foolish, the affair was over and done with, it was a fait accompli. More importantly, my husband had come back to me and I think both of us had learnt a great deal from this mishap.

Tara got up and walked away from Rohit further into the garden.

There were fresh flowers strewn all over the ground, some half submerged in the wet mud, some trampled over while yet others were still alive, but barely, gasping for breath still beautiful despite being so badly bruised. Many of the gladioli had survived the night's onslaught and she gently touched the oyster white, vibrant yellow and pale pink stems. The frangipani glowed with luninosity and the roses, delicately coated with dew, were still perfectly formed and their scented bodies hung heavily in the air.

MINA

31

Mina had never felt so good. She could feel the adrenalin course through her veins. She had just been voted the most famous businesswoman of the year. She had finally done it. After all the years of struggle true recognition was coming her way and how. . . .

Talented and determined, she would have succeeded in both the India's, but her rise was far more meteoric in the new era. There was an openness, more of an entrepreneurial spirit that dominated and allowed many more to make their fortunes. She was a true representative of the urban Indian woman today. She wanted a home but she was not just a homebody. She was as good as the next man if not better and was out to prove it.

The change had to do with the arrival of the middle classes. Their seismic proportions could not be overlooked. Women had a lot to do with this change. They were now entering the workforce in droves, competing for jobs only men thought they had a monopoly on and thus changing the cultural mould they had existed in and also altering the family structure.

The arrival of the multinationals, the increase in world trade, improvement in global communications and privatisation all had a helping hand in creating this gargantuan group.

I saw Rani, Kishore Malhotra's wife sitting in a corner and trying hard not to bite her nails.

I sat by her wondering what I could say or do to help. Everyone knew her problem. Rani was a very young thirty-three and totally insecure. She wanted to end her marriage but didn't know how to go about it. She was financially dependent on her husband who she knew would never give her a penny. Her in-laws would be only too happy to see the last of her. Her own parents would hardly welcome her back with open arms for it had been such a relief when she had finally left in the first place. And her brothers and sisters were too involved in their own lives to worry about hers. No, there was no one she could turn to. She would have to make a go of it alone. An unhappy marriage had her trapped in nothingness. No feelings were involved. From ecstasy it had moved to indifference and then nothing. But now the casual acceptance, that resignation of everything had given way to a smouldering bitterness and anger. The impetus to do something, to break free was burning inside her and she knew she could no longer remain stagnant.

But what was she to do? It kept coming back to one thing. She had to find another man. She felt trapped and useless. And angry that despite everything she needed another man to help her out of the mess she was in. There did not seem to be any other alternative. She was not qualified for any job and any kind of education at this stage required further money. But who was to say that the next guy would not be just as bad if not worse?

"What are you thinking?" Rani asked. "I'm thinking about you, my dear. Just thinking about you," said Mina. "And what grand conclusion have you come to?" Rani said teasingly.

"Why don't you come and work with me?" Mina said. "I would love to have someone I like and trust working beside me and it would do you a world of good to get out of the house, a chance to earn some money of your own which would give you the financial independence and security that you need."

"Congratulations, congratulations to the most famous designer," shouted Mrs Singh, the hostess from across the room.

She came waddling towards me, puffing heavily and almost out of breath. She wanted to be the first to greet me and the effort had cost her dearly. By the time she came close to me, she could barely say anything.

I took her to one side of the room and let her regain her composure. All around us there was much laughter, the babble of voices and the clink of glasses.

"My dear Mina," she said with great effort. In between her great gulps of breath it sounded like *'Maaa dearrr Mmmina.'* I made a great effort not to laugh and replied at once. "Yes my dear Mrs Singh."

"I am so proud of you, so very very proud of you. To have received such a distinguished award at such a young age is truly remarkable. But then I always knew you were an exceptionally gifted designer." When there was no response from me, she nudged me with one of her meaty elbows, "haven't I always said you were a great designer?"

I had been looking around for someone to rescue me but answered immediately in the affirmative, "Yes you have always been consistent in your support."

She looked at me for a moment to see if I was mocking her but then decided otherwise and launched headlong into a monologue.

The raucous laughter from a group close by floated around us and much to my relief broke the monologue.

I looked to see what was happening. Anil, my ex-husband, looking like a cheap hoodlum with a silk shirt open to his waist, excessively tight pants and numerous rings on his fingers and a gold chain round his neck was surrounded by a group of toadies I recognised from earlier times. He had his hands around the necks of two giggling girls, scantily clad, while another girl was putting a glass to his lips. He spouted abuse the speed of an electric train between talk of unrequited love and betrayal. He was well on the way to getting drunk and I knew from past experience his behaviour would deteriorate accordingly.

Rati Kumar, came and sat by me. I could not believe it when she told me she was pregnant again. Her husband, Nikhil was a notorious womaniser whose exploits were well-documented and yet she continued having his children as if he was devoted to her. This was her fourth in five years. In this day and age it was ludicrous! She was the pleasant and well meaning type who thought the sun shone out of her husband. She had no idea that his regular nights out with the boys was a cover to date and bed all types of young things whose morals belonged to the new generation where being a virgin was considered "uncool" and meant you had not been able to adapt to the fast-paced changes around you. These types of women eventually settled down and got married and acted out the whole scene, or if they were lucky they found men like themselves who had done it all and marriage certainly was not going to stop either party.

Rati was such an innocent and went around telling everyone her husband needed his space. Or maybe she knew what was really going on and this was her way of coming to terms with the pain, of assuaging some of the betrayal she felt. But whichever way you looked at it, he was making a fool of her and somewhere down the line, she was going to hurt a lot more.

The way some men treated women thought Mina, was degrading. They pawed them liberally believing the age-old adage that they were only good for one thing. Their wives were pallid creatures who never batted their heavy eyelids when their husbands were found bad mouthing or lecherously eyeing their own species. One of them was attempting to express her point of view on the recent political upheavals around the world and was barely being listened to. Most of the men had amused looks on their faces, some were openly smirking, while others were not even giving her the courtesy of listening. They were talking among themselves and quite loudly. Men, she thought to herself in disgust. They were all the same. They posed as straight but the straighter they were, the more devious their activities.

"Nikhil has that type of personality Mina. He needs to be alone at times or go out with his friends when the need arises. You know what I mean? I cannot be with him all the time. It gets too much for him." Mina did not mince her words. "Rati, how can you be so deliberately naïve, so obtusely blind to the truth?"

Rati was looking particularly attractive in a peach and gold *salwar kameez* with a multicoloured *dupatta*. Her initial smile disappeared abruptly to be replaced by a worried expression that one had come to associate with her.

"What do you mean?" Without waiting for an answer, she replied to the question herself. "I might appear foolish to many people but this is the only way I know to preserve my sanity."

They both helped themselves to drinks from a passing waiter. It was a popular white wine called South of France, that was made locally. It had a pleasant texture and unlike the very cheap wines it did not leave a bad after taste. More importantly, it was reasonably priced. At Rs 300 for a bottle its reach was considerable.

Mina sipped the wine slowly mulling over what Rati

had just said. Then choosing her words carefully, she apologised to Rati for being so inconsiderate and told her she only had her best interests at heart.

She admired the fact that Rati did not launch into a maudlin diatribe of self-pity. Nor did she choose to explain herself at length. Quietly and with great dignity she said, "I love Nikhil and know that there is much that is wrong, much that needs to be corrected. I appear weak and foolish, but each circumstance has its own unique features and mine need to be handled this way. I can only thank you for your concern and assure you that I am fine but please do not be deceived by what you see."

I felt correctly chastised and decided against saying anything further. Privately however, I felt that men in general were treated too well by women and women like Rati deserved better.

There was a palpable shift in attitude among the younger generation. One could see it in the many wide-eyed damsels, confident, sharp and aggressive, who were smart if not smarter than many men and refused to be treated with anything less than they deserved. Today, a certain equality at work and a growing independence had a lot to do with the change in attitudes and the mind. Thus they could not be taken lightly.

32

Anil could see Mina looking at him with disgust and it made him shout even louder.

She had let him down. She thought she was better than him and had started bossing him around. She no longer loved him. Taking another swig of his drink he thought back to the time when she told him she wanted a divorce.

I did not want to turn my back on her. All the memories from the past came flashing past me. Her huge eyes staring out of her face, her lips trembling and hands clenching and unclenching themselves in frustration. Other thoughts came to mind. How she had stood by me in my time of need when nobody else would, her encouragement and painful sacrifices up the ladder of success. And now, after all that, we had come to this? How could I even think of leaving her.

I refused to see the writing on the wall. Defeat was staring me in the face but I closed my mind to it. I was determined to try again, to win her back if possible and the enormity of the situation suddenly made itself clear to me. From a great distance, I heard her answer and knew I had lost. My mind had gone blank and I felt a coolness in my veins. I felt nothing for a few moments and then like burning lava I felt the heat move all over me, scalding my brain, penetrating my insides. I was in pain and intense agony and I thought I was burning in hell.

Mina remembered too. I had to fight this overwhelming urge to slap him on his face and wipe that stupid smirk off his face. But I controlled myself and instead had to listen to him blabbering about women, fidelity and love.

Let me start from the begnning as I am sure you are getting confused. Anil and I worked in the same export house. We started out at the same time having graduated from the same college. We didn't know each other then but working in close proximity, we found ourselves drawn to each other.

W would discuss fabrics, new designs and our eventual hopes over our shared sandwiches and packed lunches. These lunches slowly led to dinners, first on the premise that we wanted to discuss work and then later because we wanted to be together.

He proposed to me after six months of heavy petting and two weeks of syrupy affection that had me panting with longing for the much awaited question.

"Mina, you are beautiful and talented, far more talented than I will ever be, you are everything a man could wish for. Say, you'll marry me."

It was not the most original of speeches nor was it very romantic. He proposed while I was sitting on the pot concentrating on shaking my bowels which had refused to go into action during the last few days. I was floored by his humility and honesty not realising it was the last time I would ever hear him acknowledge my talent.

I just stared at him, the answer written all over my face and giving up on my stubborn body parts, I rushed to embrace him, stars in my eyes, the happiest girl on earth.

Why, I often wondered did I ever agree to marry him? It is not that he did not have any sterling qualities because he did, otherwise I could never have been attracted to him in the first place. But at that moment when he asked me to marry him, I could think of nothing but my good fortune.

My fortune started to sag soon after we got married.

We had decided after much prodding on my part to go into business on our own. After all the fastest selling designs were ours and I was sure together we could make a success of it.

"If we want to make a name for ourselves, we have to branch out on our own. And I'm sure most of the clients will come to us since they like our clothes." He was hesitant, even scared and started blubbering about finances, risks, loyalty but I cut him short. I wanted this more than anything else and not even Anil was going to stop me.

We arranged the finance or rather I should say I raised it because the bank was giving the money to us based on most of my designs. I never saw it then but Anil begrudged me that little victory and kept his petty grievances stored away. As each successive failure came the inevitable frustrations and unhappiness grew and festered till it overtook him completely and signalled the end of our marriage.

But that was much later. At first we were both ecstatic. It was every hard work, though setting up a new business from scratch and trying to make a name in the face of immense competition. We would be working well into the night, often sleeping a few hours at the office because it didn't make sense going home. But I repeat it was really hard work. We had to start everything from scratch. A place, people to work with us, new designs, fabrics, contacts, the whole lot. Eventually after almost nine months of back-breaking work, we got our first order. I still remember that day. Anil came waving this piece of paper yelling at the top of his voice, "we did it!, we did it!" He picked me up in his arms and swirled me around, he could barely get the words out. It was a big order and it was a start and we made sure we executed it to perfection.

After that there was no looking back but the cracks in

our marriage grew as did the cracks in our work until finally it just blew up in my face.

They used to be happy when they were working so closely together and then when they had won their first big export order, they felt nothing could stop them now. She could still see it all in her mind. Anil had come rushing to the workshop, had shouted all the way from the *gully* till the whole *mohalla* knew. By the time he had reached the room he had a whole fan following. He had taken her in his arms and whirled her around and around. "Put me down, put me down, everyone is looking," she had screamed. But of course he was beyond hearing.

When eventually he had calmed down a bit, they discussed how they were going to handle such a big order. They didn't have the capacity, the workers, the money, nothing. From a few such high moments, he suddenly came down. But she refused to give in. They had got the order. This was their lucky break and they would have to do it. And they did get there. She had nearly killed herself with the effort. Anil would go through highs and lows. When everything was going well, he would be in a genial mood but if a sample did not prove good enough and was sent back or a design had to be repeated, he would get completely derailed and collapse in depression.

Gradually, she began taking more and more upon herself without Anil really ever holding up his own end. He still thought of himself as the boss and although he acknowledged her help, he saw himself as the prime mover behind the whole scheme. Not that she minded. Still it irked her now and then when Anil's views were sought when she knew in a few minutes he would look to her for guidance. But she couldn't complain. After that order there had been no looking back.

But their personal life got worse. There was something missing. Perhaps it was that Anil had started taking her too much for granted. Taking a couple of decisions without her compliance and getting it all wrong but no, it was not really that. It started in the pit of her stomach and by the end it had developed into a huge heartache.

I was constantly tired, finding that increasingly I was carrying the enormous burden of the work on my shoulders. Anil was physically there, but he was usually drunk, uncooperative and sullen and spitefully making changes about designs just because I had initiated them. I could no longer talk to him and on the rare occasions that I did, it ended in maudlin self-pity for himself that disgusted me and drew me further away.

We began arguing about everything. Before we got married, we used to argue but it was philosophical arguments about the current state of the economy, people we liked or disliked, magazines we subscribed to, design points and the kinds of cuisine to eat.

After we got married it seemed to change right away. It was like we were in one slot before and another one now. Only I did not see why it should be that way. I felt we were both equal but he was always imposing his views on me: "Mina likes this too," about a record I particularly disliked but he loved or "She agrees with me completely" about a fellow competitor who I thought was talented but Anil ran down at the slightest provocation. Initially it was silly statements like this which I would rectify or we would argue about and make up. I did the making up. I hated swollen faces and fights hanging in the air. But Anil was different, he would carry a grudge for days and could go without talking while hurting me terribly in the process. But he was impervious to it all.

Soon all our fights were about one thing. Our work. He never agreed to anything I said, he was always changing my designs with his own improvisations which just didn't work and was forever humiliating me in front of others. He was often sidelined and he took out his fears and insecurities on me. I tried to cope by letting him do more of the designing and me the running of the factory but it was a disaster. We lost two of our most loyal customers and I knew I had to put a stop to it especially when the management came pleading to me.

Anil always drank, but initially he was more of a social drinker. However, after this incident, the bottle became his best friend. And replaced me as both companion and wife. He started having sycophants around him, going to five-star hotels and running up enormous bills. Sleazy women were always with him. It was pathetic, the depths to which he sank because of his own inabilities.

I tried to reason with him telling him to run the business side of things, something he was surprisingly good at, but he did not bother to hear me out. He felt I wanted to eclipse his talent by keeping him in the background.

Remember, you can only fight so much but you cannot let it destrory you. And I managed to save myself just in time before I could have been "a has been".

We'd fight about the most trivial things because there was so much that was being unsaid. Let me tell you what our fights were like.

"It's very hot," I would say.

"Sorry, didn't hear that," he would say cocking his ear in a deliberate manner designed to infuriate.

"I said it's very hot, can you please put the

airconditioner on?" Anil loved the heat and even in the sweltering summer months the fan was the most he could bear. I, of course, like any other normal person had to turn the airconditioner on when the mercury touched over 40 degrees.

He would rise with exaggerated calm and with an infinite slowness of manner switch on the airconditioner. This pretence infuriated me all the more and with temperatures boiling all around its no wonder the pretence soon faded and we started to fight.

He would them move to the farthest point of the room and make himself into a little bundle as if to say, "fine have it your way. All I need is a little corner for myself."

He's pushing me, he is trying my patience and goading me into a fight. I resist for a while and let the cool air breathe its magic on me.

After a time he gets himself a blanket and a duvet. He does not need both but he's just proving a point. He then proceeds to hum some ridiculous tune under his breath lowering his voice when I look at him and then increasing the sound, tempo, beat. . .everything . . . when I turn away.

By now my nerves have reached fever pitch and I can't stand it any more. I turn off the air-conditioner but he goes and puts it back on.

"Don't put the air-conditioner off because of me. So what if I'm freezing, I'll just take an extra blanket."

"Why do you have to be so damn selfish?" I ask him.

He raises his eyebrows in a manner I used to find sexy but now looks depressing and affected. "Selfish. Look whose calling who selfish!"

"Why do you always have to fight about everything?"

He puts aside a design he's been drawing and makes a great pretence of innocence.

"Fight and me!" He makes a big thing about shrugging his shoulders.

I feel myself boil inside, I want to throw something at him and wipe that smug look off his face but I restrain myself. I feel an acute sense of defeat and just look at him blankly.

"Why do we fight like this?. . . What has happened to both of us? It used not to be this way."

"That's because you never tried to upstage me. Always trying to show you are better than me, your work is better than mine. Well its not..." He got up suddenly and threw his work in my face. "You are not the only one whose good."

All this shouting, the pent up emotions, frustrations at work, everything comes to a head and I start to cry. That infuriates him even more. He thinks I am using this feminine ploy when all else has failed. What he does not realise is that I am crying for the both of us. I do not force the tears out and hope he will stop shouting and we'll patch up the fight before there is nothing left to patch up. I'm crying for what was and what could have been.

Human beings are strange creatures. We always try to hide ourselves, our true selves, our emotions for fear of exposing ourselves. Anil and I were fighting without addressing the real problem. It didn't matter if one of us felt hot and the other cold, we could have found some kind of solution but no, we continued to fight about it because we were too scared to address ourselves not realising that each fight was setting us apart. We are such prickly beings. I do not know why we were not called porcupine!

33

Anil had started taking her for granted. She felt hurt and vulnerable. And increasingly felt herself drawn towards a kind word, some show of sympathy which was very unlike herself. She prided herself on her strength and would flick away condescendingly those who were too syrupy, too false. But lately, she had fallen into the trap. She had just given a huge order to a young and upcoming designer whom she ordinarily couldn't stand but lately she actually began looking forward to his smooth brand of flowery compliments and exaggerated flattery. It soothed her bruised ego. And why not? She was in charge after all. Anil did not really know anything.

She sat down with a sigh. She felt terribly alone. For a moment it all seemed so unfair. She had worked her guts out and instead of reaping the benefits together with her husband, was having to work harder while Anil, was the talk of the town with anything with legs and a wiggle.

Deepak Mehra looked at Mina covertly. He wondered who she was thinking about, he felt sure it was not about him.

She had been his ticket to the big time but he had handled it badly. In those very rare moments of insight he knew he was not at all talented and would never amount to anything but second best. There were others far more talented.

Deepak was their assistant. He had just finished his training abroad at a prestigious art and design school in New

York. He was a close friend's nephew and they welcomed the chance to help someone whose situation they had been in not too long ago.

From the moment Mina met him, she did not like him. She felt he was too arrogant and too cocky for his own good. He was filled with supreme confidence coupled with a thick skin that shielded all the barbs that were directed against him. He projected himself as the greatest talent when he was barely mediocre. "I'm going to be the most famous designer in another two years" was his favourite refrain. And there was no doubt that he would possibly achieve that goal with the backup of money and contacts. Plus he was dismissive of anyone who he considered was less than him. So he made many enemies. Anil was one of them. He did not think Deepak was good at all and instead of trying to learn from him considering that was what he was there for, he was constantly making disparaging remarks. It was surprising that Anil tolerated him.

To tell the truth, Anil put up with him because he was scared of him. He might not be the only person who believed he was mediocre but he was the only person who was not afraid to say so. Also, he was a dear friend's nephew and he owed a great deal to this friend, so he put up with him. Deepak knew this and this added to his cockiness. He went around the factory as if he owned the place, constantly making changes to designs. But nobody said anything because the changes were invariably better than the original and more often than not they were Anil's designs!

Deepak was also a flirt. Despite his coarse behaviour, he had women falling all over him. He always had something flattering to say to each one of them making them feel they were the only ones who mattered. Initially he had turned on the charm with Mina but she had witheringly told him to cut the act and behave himself if he wanted to continue working with them. After that he had never tried anything although his flattery continued unabated.

He had always had dreams of making it big. He was extremely ambitious and without a shred of conscience. Up the ladder he had befriended and dropped many on the way to get this far. But this was the ultimate staircase. And he would do anything to protect it. He realised he would probably end up having to sleep with the old hag but what the hell it was well worth the sacrifice.

And he looked at her again. She was not that bad, he thought to himself. A bit too conventional for his liking. The standard *salwar kameez,* even though it was a pretty piece from the popular looms of the Self-Employed Women's Association (SEWA). Her hair was tied back with an insipid looking rubber band. There was hardly any makeup except the obligatory kohl and lipstick. Deepak liked a bit more *pizzazz.* Trendy flairs with *kurtas,* fragrant flowing tresses and beguiling make up that was both sensual and authoritarian. Yes, he would definitely have to do something about the "look". Especially as they were going to be an item. He was very sure about that.

If she had known what was going through his mind at the time, she would have been appalled.

If one did things and then much later on regretted them what was the point of doing it in the first place? At that time one feels strongly about a particular issue and then later on it merges into nothingness.

Everyone thought Anil was a kind and gentle soul for he rarely had a harsh word to say to anyone. But there was another side to him, a darker side that came to the fore when he drank too much. At that time he was particularly nasty and even violent.

When had he started drinking? Well, as I said before he had always done so in moderation. You know, the obligatory glass of beer or whisky at a party but the glass remained with him during the entire evening. There were no refills. Actually I can see that his drinking problem started as he ascended the ladder to fame. There were obviously more parties and more people to meet, nights got longer and longer and then lunch meetings became part of the pattern. As he got better known, he acquired new friends who plied him with the stuff and refused to take no for an answer. But I have to honestly say that was not the only reason. He had problems with me. In his heart he knew I was better than him and although I never let him or anyone else be aware of it, it came between us. It had to come to the fore eventually. And he became increasingly bitter as the truth ate inside him. And as I got more accolades so Anil became even more jealous, the bitterness churning itself inside him, burning and rancid. His temper became worse and along with it he developed a cruel tongue.

"Why are you behaving like such a martyr, pretending I am as good as you, as talented as you when you and everyone knows I will never be as creative as you. You think I don't know that you and your friends are laughing behind my back, making fun of my designs and then pretending in front of me that they are actually good? You think I don't know. Well, I do. You are such a damned hypocrite. . . ."

This kind of paranoia and self-pity inevitably let to a show down replete with all kinds of coarse language and choice abuse that got more coarse in proportion to the drink in his hand.

If he had kept it at that perhaps I would not have minded so much. I knew I was extremely talented and my work was recognised as such, but this only served to further fuel his jealousy. But when he started cursing my inability to have children, I knew I could only take so much and no more. In the beginning he had been so kind, so sympathetic and understanding. As one childless year drifted into another and we realised we would never have children, he had always been at my side. He just could not accept the fact that his wife was more talented than he was. His ego was bruised and like a wounded lion he set out to avenge himself.

I found myself crying a lot during those times but never in front of him. It would only give him more sadistic pleasure and another victory to notch up. After these scenes, we would sleep in separate bedrooms but then he would come crawling full of apologies and mushy one liners that made me sick. He would be extremely confident and breezy making all sorts of vows and promises to keep our marriage from going under. This was followed by confessions in which he would admit all his hang ups and jealousies. At the end he would proclaim undying love for me.

"Please forgive me, Mina. I love you so much, so passionately, so intensely, please, please give me another chance. I promise I will turn over a new leaf, the kind of husband you want, who you can look up to and respect. You are so beautiful and talented and I am not really good enough for you. I know that, but please help me to be a better person. It's just that I want to be as good as you are and I have difficulty accepting that I will never be more than a mediocre designer. Certainly never attain the kind of heights that you have. Please give me another chance, you know I cannot live without you and will do anything in my power for you."

Initially, I was so moved by his apparent emotion and sincerity, I echoed his promise. But it was just a temporary reprieve till his next bout and soon it became a pattern that left me totally unmoved. The whole thing was humiliating and I felt sad that despite all that we had achieved in life, we were desperately unhappy with each other. I had by this time abslutely no respect for the man. There was no love and except for loneliness and despair, I did not see anything in the marriage to keep us together. I decided to get a divorce.

It was not a decision I had taken lightly or in a moment of pique. It was only after several months of thinking and agonising that I finally drew upon this solution. I knew I was to lose more than Anil. After all despite the trappings of modernity, Indians had not changed all that much. A single woman is a single woman and a divorcee, well she is always prey to every kind of low life. It is as if they come creeping out of the woodwork. She is an easy target and if she is divorced it is generally understood that she is some kind of fallen creature and fair game for others. She is thus branded as a wily operator out to grab other women's husbands. And she finds herself condemned by both parties. A women who is married has a name in society, a status and respect that is accorded to her all because she bears her husband's name, never mind if her husband is a complete wastrel.

34

How Deepak and I came to be lovers was purely accidental.

Deepak walked passed, winking suggestively and I recoiled in remembered horror and repugnance.

It was late one evening well past midnight when everyone in the factory had left and just the two of them were putting the finishing touches to a particularly arduous shipment. Anil of course was at home drunk having walked out petulantly one afternoon when he was overruled on a particular suggestion.

They were both exhausted and he had just made a fresh cup of coffee for both of them when their fingers brushed each other accidentally. Perhaps she was exhausted and in no mood to go home and confront Anil with his drunken and maudlin apologies. Whatever it was, he gauged the situation, seized the moment and made his move and they were both surprised when she did not resist.

Deepak looked back at her. He wondered if she ever thought about him. He remembered the affair and the heady feeling of power he had experienced. He looked at her. She was beautiful then and now. She had closed her eyes and allowed him to do as he willed.

I was so overcome with lust and unlike my usual confident self. I was trembling as my hands tried to undo her buttons and my fingers kept slipping. She was so soft and feminine but she surprised me by her passion.

I took her twice in the space of a short time and she was a wonderful partner.

Mina thought back and actually saw her mind had closed down, she just let herself drown in the feeling of the moment. She needed those orgasms. She was so out of practice but it hardly mattered for she more than made up with her enthusiasm.

Afterwards nothing was said. Mina was appalled that she let herself go all the way, that she was so weak to succumb to a man she abhorred and who was many years her junior. She was married for god's sake. But none of that seemed to have mattered at that moment.

I was a butterfly caught in a nightmare of torrid passions, I detested my dependence on him sexually, while fascinated by the momentary high it gave me. I looked into the mirror searching for something other than the myriad reflections of myself, bestial and lustful.

Deepak wanted me all the time. His lust was no longer satiated at these nightly rendezvous. Apart from that, things had become very different and were no longer the way they used to be. To start with, I had been shy, even resistant and ferociously scared of what I was doing. Deepak, on the other hand, was gentle, understanding and always made a big show of asking me if I was comfortable. Even though I was usually miserable, I could only say "yes." However, as the affair progressed, he lost his patience and said it was about time I learnt how to be a good lover, a real woman.

I look back at myself and am surprised I did not tell him to go to hell. But I think it speaks volumes for my low self-esteem and total lack of self-confidence at that point. My relationship with Anil had left me completely demoralised. So, when Deepak said he wanted me to open myself to new ways of making love, despite my inherent nervousness, I decided to follow him and try and learn from the experience.

The new experience came the very first night after Deepak had talked about it. It was late and everyone at the factory had gone home. He walked up to me and started kissing me aggressively. He pushed me against the wall and rubbed himself hard against me. He started swearing loudly, calling me filthy names and urged me to do likewise. He wanted to hear me talk dirty. He wanted me to say words that prostitutes used to entice men, a kind of gutter language that was alien to me. He kept egging me on but I could not do it and pulled away from him.

"I cannot," I told him.

"Of course you can," he said and pulled me towards him. His caresses were now more insistent and he persisted in his entreaties.

Finally, I told him I could not say the words he wanted so desperately to hear and smile at him sweetly hoping he would understand. I was embarrassed and unsure and desperately wanted his understanding.

But a sudden metamorphosis took place. His face twisted into an ugly sneer and he unexpectedly took hold of my shoulders and shook me vigorously.

"Why can't you say them? I want to hear you say them." When I stayed silent he yelled loudly, "say them, say them," and showered a string of expletives and talked dirty. He also began knocking things around and messing up the room.

I was really scared now and did not know what to do. I began to cry. It was a silly thing to do because I should just have told him to get lost and turned him out of my room. My tears were a signal of my weakness and he took advantage of that weakness.

He pulled my clothes off and made me stand naked against the wall. He drew back and surveyed me coldly for what seemed an eternity. Then very quietly, so quietly I could almost feel the deadliness of his tone, he commanded me to say the words.

I felt humiliated by his look and disgusted by his words but before I could think of a suitable response, he slapped me hard, twice. I collapsed on the floor completely demoralised and unaware of myself as a human being with any rights or dignity. I began to grovel. I begged him to stop, to let me go, anything to get away but to no avail and finally I said the words he was so adamant to hear from my lips.

After that, I degraded myself repeatedly. Whenever he wanted me I was there, like a whore pliable in his hands, at his mercy, his slightest command and I would do his bidding. It was really quite pathetic.

Sometimes, we played games. I had to beg him to touch me and he would refuse: I would then have to dance for him, cajole, entice him through intimate gestures that got intensely whorish, whipping up foul language that excited him. At other times, he made me touch myself in the most intimate manner while he watched. Often, without warning, he would attack me from behind. If was painful and nauseating but I was caught in his bestiality, unable to break free.

At other times, he would hurl abuse and compare me to other women he had bedded. I was always found wanting, no matter how low I stooped for him. On one occasion, he even suggested I club together with another girl friend of his so he could watch. But he did not mention it again. He sensed my revulsion and probably realised it was insurmountable.

35

When I look back on that time, and it is not often that I do for I have tried to blot it completely out of my mind, I cannot understand how I let myself fall to such depths of degradation. I console myself and say it is because I sank so low that I have managed to pull myself up and emerge a stronger person.

I am not explaining things to you in detail so you sympathise with me. Indeed, I do not expect any sympathy, just your understanding. I needed to tell you how it really was so you know what it is like to be held captive, your mind devoid of any consciousness, simply giving in to a force that is stronger than you but at the same time you know is evil.

The affair lasted for a few months. Mina was ashamed of herself but seemed to have no control, while Deepak continued to be his cocky self, even worse if that was possible. Matters came to a head when she heard Deepak bragging about it over the phone.

"Everything's under control, do not worry. For all practical purposes I am the boss. Pumping the wife. She's head over heels in love with me, can't do without me. You just wait and see. Soon I'll take over the whole unit."

Mina was shaking uncontrollably when she heard this. She stood rooted to the spot as the rest of the conversation came across. "Her husband is a total wimp. He's just no good, no talent at all. She is very good," he admitted reluctantly into the phone. "But I am better than her and she needs me both ways. I've got the whole thing signed and sealed."

Mina saw Deepak looking at her and stared back. He

smiled knowingly and then raised his glass in a toast and tossed the contents back.

Mina looked at his hand. It was a big squarish hand and, went well with the rest of him. She had never noticed how well manicured his nails were. They were clipped down to the ends and there was a glint on the surface which suggested he indulged in regular manicures. How strange she thought. I never would have imagined being attracted to someone who spent time in a beauty saloon. She had rather fixed ideas about that. She liked a man who was well groomed but imagining someone spending hours on end in a beauty parlour did not seem right to her. She herself considered it a waste of time and her regular one hour a week at the parlour was often torture.

His movements were controlled suggesting hidden strength and yet graceful denoting a fluidity that was not obviously apparent. As he raised his glass in the air the thought that leapt to mind was one of a leopard she had seen on television, strong and dangerous, with an intent of purpose that was hidden behind immense grace and swift footedness.

Much later on when she left him, she realised the relationship could never have got off the ground with someone whose hands bothered her and appeared to be stalking her for the final kill.

That night she had decided to fire him. True he had made himself indispensable by wiggling his way into every major decision that needed to be made, making friends with important suppliers but still she could do without him.

He had swaggered into the factory at around midday as if he owned the place. I watched him from my office. The blinds had not been pulled down and I had a clear view of him. He was wearing a white shirt with white trousers and can you believe it – white shoes! On one writst he sported a thick gold bracelet and most of his fingers seemed to have rings on them. His shirt was almost open till his navel and another gold bauble glittered through. His hair was unruly and unkempt. He whistled as he walked towards the office; alsolutely sure of himself and his charms. He looked utterly *filmi* and not unlike Jeetender, the Hindi film hero of yesteryears. I watched him with distaste and wondered why I had never seen him like this.

Deepak saw the flitting emotions across Mina's face and changed his mind about talking to her. Instead he concentrated his charms on a woman who had just walked in.

She looked great in a black outfit. Stunning actually and I was literally quite awe-struck for a few moments. I had first thought she was much younger than her husband but now I saw that she was probably the same age and really the impression of youth was all a matter of clever dressing. She was immaculately made up and most of the tell tale signs of a woman past her menopause had been carefully hidden. Indeed, if it wasn't for the wrinkles on her neck or the puffed and slightly gnarled hands it would have been difficult to tell her age. Her figure was quite something and was probably one of her best features and she obviously knew it because the black dress clung to her curves like a second body. She was interesting and enigmatic. I decided I was going to spend some time trying to unravel the mystery.

After firing Deepak, Mina realised she had to leave Anil. He was the cause of all her unhappiness.

Then one day, just like that I ended it all. The affair and its implications had opened my eyes. Neither men were worthy of me. I got home one evening at two o'clock in the morning, bone tired and looking forward to nothing other than crawling into bed. My bedroom, that I took such pride in, that I had decorated with such enthusiasm was altered beyond recognition. Anil had written all over my pristine walls with lipstick, actually broken two of my best crystal vases and smashed a few family pictures. One of the curtains had been torn from its hinges and the exotic Mexican rug I had bought on one of my trips had been cut, the scissors still lying midway as if it had proved too much for its attacker. And my bed was occupied by this dirty, dishevelled drunk who I barely recognised as my husband. It was a normal scene that I should have become familiar with but suddenly it all seemed too much. It wedged itself right inside my gut and I knew it was the last time he would sleep in my house.

I remember kicking him viciously but to no avail. He was too drunk to feel anything and apart from mumbling incoherently, he simply lay there. After a few more kicks, I felt better and sat down opposite him. I looked at his face, softer and unlined in repose and wondered where we had gone wrong. Things had been so good between us initially. We could have had a great life together. But no, no it was not to be. Petty jealousy and human insecurities were sometimes hard to bridge. The mind was a powerful instrument and once it had chosen a particular path it was difficult though not impossible to turn back. Unfortunately, Anil's mind had been set on its course and no amount of reasoning could bring it back to its original path.

Mina wished both Deepak and Anil were not at the party. But she knew she had to get used to seeing them. She hated remembering.

When we signed the divorce papers, I felt a vacuum, and the sense of loss was acute. I cried till there were no tears left. My head ached with thousands of darting drums pounding at its temples, my throat was dry and I longed to lose myself in slumber that seemed to have become a recent stranger.

For a long long time, I kept thinking about my marriage; five unbearably long years trying hard to make someone else happy and sacrificing myself in the process. I groaned loudly and turned my side on the bed wishing I could control my mind and blank out all the hurt and disillusionment.

I felt a change within myself. I could not help it. For a time I had become indifferent. Indifferent to those around me. Petty courtesies no longer came easily and instead people were met with sudden silences, vague monosyllabic answers and curt withdrawal.

As each of my friends came to console me, I told them different things about Anil but they were all true, the sum part that made up the whole. And I did not realise it at that time but as I talked about my feelings with different people, I was opening my wounds and allowing them to heal.

With my parents I was quiet and subdued, I controlled my tears for I knew it would upset them greatly. I told them what a fool I had been to have married someone so obviously insecure and emotionally immature. I felt we had all been betrayed.

To my friend, Arundhati, I spoke from the depths of my heart when I told her that living with Anil was unbearable and without him was the same. So perhaps I should go back to him.

She was horrified and said so. "Go back and do what? Live a life of intense depression, self-pity and emotional blackmail? Face up to it, the man is a wastrel and you were too good for him."

"I love him, I miss him terribly. I need him and he needs me. Maybe he can change."

But I knew deep within me that it could never happen.

Too much had happened and while there was no going back there was no going forward. The break had been effected and had to continue. Any other way would be to cheat oneself.

I went around with a dull ache lodged in my heart that sometimes burned inside me and felt as if someone was throwing red hot chillies on my open wound.

When my thoughts turned to revenge and I told Tara I wanted to pull him apart like a piece of chicken, wham! One buttock this end and the other that end, I didn't realise how much I was healing. Just saying it gave me a feeling of intense satisfaction.

I could just imagine his face as he looked down at his body to find it broken in half. I found myself in splits just thinking about Anil as a *tandoori* chicken!

Jai, the reputed journalist, was listening to our hostess, Mrs Singh tell him about her recently acquired painting. He was not at all interested but stayed put nevertheless while his eyes darted around the room. Our eyes locked and we both smiled. He almost managed to excuse himself but Mrs Singh had not finished and after she gave me a dirty look, put her elbow in his and dragged him to another part of the room.

He was small and always ushaven. He wore a crumpled *kurta* no matter where you met him, his feet were perpetually out of his sandals which did not appear at all comfortable and when you asked him he would say as much. His *jhola* contained vast amounts of trivia, all dirty and old looking. He was to be found always chewing a *paan* and cleaning his mouth with a sodden handkerchief. Many looked upon him with distaste and he produced quite a shudder when he was invited to some socialite evening or the other. In fact it was quite amusing to see some society lady having to fawn on him because he was a powerful journalist. He could make or break a person depending on how he wrote the column the next morning. In fact he could be extremely embarrassing. On one occasion, I heard him tell a powerful industrialist's wife: "That dress does nothing for you. The resemblance between you and a ripe juicy tomato is not far off." Another time his loud voice boomed across a room consisting of more than a hundred people: "Don't try and pretend that you are a friend of mine. We hardly know each other and the only reason you bother to talk to me is because you are planning to take your company public and you need all the publicity you can get. Unfortunately a skunk will always remain a skunk and I have a keen sense of smell."

But when one saw beyond all this, he had one of the sweetest smiles, enough to melt the hearts of the toughest editors.

He was at the height of his success. He got all the plum assignments, had his byline written out in bold and commanded an impressive salary along with the more than requisite perks. Only the very top and the very best journalists got to where he had. The majority are paid low wages but nevertheless are slaves to their jobs, because of the status and prestige and for some even excitement of the job.

Everyone knew Jai was in town. You knew because of the buzz that surrounded him. He had taken to using gel, lots of it. In the sweltering summer months he was seen dripping sweat and gel while mosquitoes and flies had a party.

Jai always had people around him. Be it in his office, his house or a dinner party there was no doubt who was holding court. The people who surrounded him were mainly aspiring journalists who hung on to his every word, businessmen who needed something favourable written about them, politicians currently in power and out and some flatterers who lapped up his every word.

Everywhere he went he was the centre of attention. A word from him could make that all important difference. His social calendar was inundated with invitations to exclusive parties, previews and political meetings. His restaurant bills were always met, the exclusive use of some fancy car or the other replete with dark windows and one digit number plate.

There was no doubt he had arrived. And how. No one knew his background. The air of power that surrounded him precluded too many questions. In fact the air of superiority and nonchalance coupled with good living were all carefully cultivated images. Jai hailed from a mediocre background. His father was a mechanic and his mother sewed women's sari blouses. Right from the beginning he had a distaste for his background. Of his five brothers, he was the most ambitious and believed there was another better world for him which they could not even fathom.

His rise had been spectacular. With his fierce determination, hard work and quick intelligence coupled with an uncanny sense of gauging people's weaknesses, his rise to the top had been assured.

He had known about Mina's affair with Deepak and had warned her about him. Although she valued his opinion, she had not listened to him. She had not listened to anyone else, either.

Those months after our divorce were ones where I did a lot of soul searching. Anil had always been wrong for me but I had not listened to my parents and friends when they had tried to point out his obvious flaws. I had listened to my heart but without giving it the correct information. I had suppressed things about him that I did not like preferring to gloss over them and magnify those that I did.

My mother's favourite refrain was "your mother is your

best friend. You will always do your own thing but after many rounds will come back to what your mother told you in the first place." Her favourite phrase was an analogy with a tree: "If you listen to your mother you will grow tall and straight but if you do not heed her advice the tree would bend from the pressure of the wind and become gnarled and knotty." And she was right. She had warned me about Anil, how I wish to God I had listened to her. I felt emotionally drained and worse, a failure.

36

I felt Shekhar looking at me from across the room and I moved towards him. As I returned his look, I felt a great surge of happiness course through my veins and I flashed a smile that probably looked idiotic to an onlooker. But I did not care any more about appearances.

It had only been a few minutes since we parted but still I kissed him enthusiastically. Onlookers made faces and raised their eyebrows but I was not concerned in the slightest.

"I missed you sweetheart. Are you having a good time?" she asked lovingly. Shekhar smiled gently. "Yes darling, I am at the moment. How about you? Are you enjoying yourself?"

He was so kind and considerate. He was always more interested in my well-being, always putting my feelings first. I had blossomed under his loving care and could not imagine a life without his tender ministrations. "I love you Shekhar," Mina said spontaneously and hugged him tight, squeezing his huge frame as hard as she could.

She had broken free from the confines that conventionality imposed upon her. She could be found singing to herself at different times and with no sense of embarrassment or trepidation, she would break out in full gusto. Shekhar had done that to her. Made her totally whole.

The moments of shared confidences were brief. She was so reticent, she never said anything and even though I was her closest friend, I was never privy to her intimacy.

I was naturally inquisitive but when it came to friends nothing could hold me back. I would try and squeeze all the juice possible not with any malicious motive in mind but I just had to know. It made me feel something, kinship perhaps.

"If you had a chance again would you marry your husband?" I once asked her nonchalantly while we were sunning ourselves oblivious to everything around us except getting maximum enjoyment out of the moment.

She looked at me directly for a moment and then said, "No".

She was quiet for a while and I decided not to impinge on her thoughts and keep my questions in check for the moment. After a while, she spoke again. "I married Avinash when I was only seventeen. It was my mother's decision. I saw him alone twice after that, he seemed pleasant enough and I said 'yes'. Actually, even if I had said 'no' it would have made little difference. My parents had found this match to be of their standing in society and there was no way it was not going to happen. The fact that I was so young was immaterial, after all many girls from our families marry at that age."

Mina learned from the odd remark dropped unconsciously what it was like to be Mrs Arundhati Diwan, the difficulties with her mother-in-law and slowly the realisation that the marriage was nothing but a sham.

Arundhati was initially guarded about her past and never volunteered any information. But as the friendship grew so did the trust and slowly she started confiding small incidents with less reluctance and more ease.

Mina knew she was privileged to have a friend such as Arundhati. She was a deep person who formed attachments with difficulty unlike herself but would be loyal unto death. She saw a side of Arundhati that not many did. She loved to be tickled and giggled like a child, her soft laughter carrying a note of intense joy. She was a great ice-cream fan and when she was together with her son eating an ice-cream, there was no difference between the two. She was intensely affectionate, you had only to say something once and no matter how difficult the task, she would make sure it was done. She expected nothing in return and never asked. She was afraid of rejection and yet gave of herself totally. Yet, this was all in private. In public, Arundhati became another person and Mina felt sad that the hurt and betrayal in her life had penetrated so deeply. She was a friend like no other and in a society that was grasping and shallow they both knew they were lucky to find each other.

I saw Rusi Chinoy approach Arundhati and knew she was well looked after. He was a delightful man and Arundhati had a soft spot for him.

I turned towards Shekhar. The cliched phrase, "the course of true love never did run smoothly," came to mind. Although I was now, after a failed first marriage and a disastrous affair with Deepak, happily married to Shekhar. We had our share of problems to contend with.

The problem with being married to an older or elderly man is that you have to suffer for the discrepancy in your ages. He would invariably become morose or uptight when he saw you enjoying yourself with someone your own age. It made him all the more possessive and he tended to be around you just when you did not want him hovering over you. It is always an uncomfortable feeling to have someone showing his possession of you when you do not even want him there.

Shekhar had a large and varied circle of friends but what was surprising or perhaps not really was that not one of then was under the age of forty-five.

Mina squeezed Shekhar's arm lovingly and he smiled seeming to understand the love in that pressurised touch.

37

I constantly worried about my advanced age and the growing disparity between us. I never thought I would feel this way. I always despised other men who seemed to be hopelessely devoted to their much younger wives and carried on like love-sick puppies but to my consternation, I now found myself in the same state. The green-eyed monster was rearing itself in my mind and I was both astonished and upset that I of all people should succumb to an emotion as base as jealousy.

Mina was amazed at my feeling when I told her I wished I was quite a few years younger. "Why, what difference would that make? It is all in the mind. You are exactly what I wanted, not some hot stud who thinks of nothing else but himself."

Before I could stop, I found myself asking anxiously, "are you sure?"

She looked at me tenderly. "You are the man I married and I will always love you despite your silly thoughts."

"I. . . hope so."

The uncertainty and sadness must have reached her. For she immediately came towards me and kissed me with great love. "Please believe me. Marrying you is like a dream come true for me. You are everything I wanted in a man. You have made me incredibly happy these past few months, it is like I have been born again. How can you even think I will stop loving you because you are older than me? It is totally immaterial to the kind of feelings we have for each other. Do not insult what we have because of your age."

And looking at her, so small and so earnest, I knew

what she said was true. After all, it was better to cherish and enjoy what we had than worry about the differences in our ages. "I love you very much," I said and at that moment age did not matter; we were just two people joined together for as long as our love survived.

Shekhar was almost sixty by the time we were married and I being much much younger, all kinds of remarks were made about us. The comments were never very complimentary and had a lot to do with doddering old men who made fools of themselves and young girls, young enough to be their daughters capturing older men's fancies all because of youth. But I never really thought about Shekhar's age. He did though, a lot. He was resentful of it and each day was another reminder of how life was passing by and that he was getting older. He was who he was and I liked him for that and I refused to listen to the well meaning advice that was given to me freely on every occasion possible. I wanted to marry him and that was all there was to it.

Shekhar looked at Mina tenderly. What happiness this woman had given him. Sometimes he could not believe that life could have dealt him such good cards; twice. He took Mina's hand in his wanting to feel her skin close to his and kissed it gently. She looked at him. There was no need to explain. She understood the feeling implicitly.

38

Shekhar was a big man, tall and well built with muscles that would have done a younger man proud. I went completely by the image of beef and brawn even though I knew the real Shekhar and expected our love-making to be good but not exceptional. I was wrong. Oh how wrong! The chemistry between us was magic. He was tender and loving in his manner towards me and I had expected the same from his love-making. But he showed a different side when we got into bed. Although he did care about my feelings and made sure I was enjoying his attention every bit as much as he did, he was no mild lover. He was passionate and fiery, our love-making was tumultuous and tempestuous, he tore my inhibitions, he examined every tiny part of me minutely, both my physical being and the inner me that I kept hidden deep inside me. With him I was fully exposed, there was no wall separating us. When I looked at him, I saw only myself.

When our bodies meet there is no holding back. There is an instant ease that banishes any awkwardness, and all inhibitions. How do I explain the feeling to you? There was a complete meshing of two individuals who knew each other and yet . . . yet were still exploring. We were as one but, but ummm . . . still plundering the unknown!

With Anil, I experienced the sweet awakening of first love, the blissful yearnings of the uninitiated who was still wet behind the ears and does not know better. My relationship with Deepak, however, was volatile, exaggerated and ultimately painful. With him, there is no doubt that I scaled great heights of passion but I also experienced a tremendous amount of disillusionment and betrayal. Tinged throughout my relationship was the knowledge that the relationship in itself was rotten from the core. Of course, this feeling of committing some kind of sin was perpetually hanging over me like a bad shadow but it added another diemension to the entire relationship; a certain amount of drama that at that time made it even more exciting. Still, in the end the heartache and headache were not worth those moments of pleasure.

Making love with Shekhar after these two desperate relationships was a pleasant finale – unexpected in its intensity and gripping in its passion. I felt alive, charged with renewed vigour and intoxicated with life. The past had, however, left its mark on me but I used it to my advantage and to my great surprise with consummate ease! Initially, Shekhar was surprised at my definite expertise and innovativeness but since we were both interested in pleasing each other – the end result was all that mattered.

Between the kisses he plants everywhere on my body and his gasps for air, he murmurs sweet nothings in my ear that add to the delirious situation I am already in. "I love you, Mina. God how I love you. You are so beautiful, so wonderful, so perfect for me." Having kissed my entire body, he has now reached my feet. Each toe is inspected lovingly and then he puts them in his mouth, one by one and sucks with great feeling. The tingling sensations that envelope my entire body defy any kind of description. My toes happen to be one of my erogenous areas and Shekhar armed with this knowledge is an undoubted love-making *maestro*!

I sit quietly afraid any movement will destroy the magic at hand. Slowly, ever so gently, I feel caressed, a slow teasing that is both tortuous and delightful. The feeling gathers momentum spreading through me like a stream, touching every little nerve. The right note has been struck and I find myself enslaved with no will of my own to alter its course. My skin is aflame and the very pores of my body respond with a new intensity. The warm glow gathers momentum changing from the soothing almost hypnotic caresses of a moment ago to great tumultuous tremors that are earth shattering in intensity. A pattern has formed and there is no going back, the path is no longer curved and contoured but straight and fearless and I float sensuously away carried to a greater height by the depth of feeling.

Mrs Singh, our plump hostess, came and took Mina away, saying she wanted to introduce her to some friends. Shekhar took his drink and found a quiet spot in a corner. He was tired and closed his eyes for a moment.

It was difficult getting married again. The trauma of my wife's death all those years ago had affected both my son and me deeply. But I was lucky to have been given a second chance and I was not going to throw it away. My son and friends would just have to learn to live with it. After all, who said I could not marry again, expect love, happiness and all the joyous things in life again? People could talk, they always would irrespective, but I wasn't about to let anyone rule my life. I wanted to live it to the fullest and I was going to.

I had been a widower for many years when I met Mina. Everyone including my close friends were convinced I would remain in this state, that in fact I was happy the way things were. Little did they realise that the opposite was the case. I had long since got over the pain and anguish that death brings for a loved one. The memory was now all but blurred and was no comfort on those cold and long winter nights. After all, one cannot talk to a memory, or hold a memory or warm one's bed with a memory. This is not to say there was a dearth of women. There wasn't, but sexual pleasure was no longer the ultimate as it had been in my hey day. And I was no fool nor a spring chicken. I realised that most of these women found me attractive because of my name, my wealth and social position. Take that away and even though I say so myself, I was still a good looking man but most of these women would drop me like a hot potato. Now I was looking for a woman who could hold my mind as well as pleasure me in bed. Such a woman was Mina.

I didn't think I would be fortunate enough to find love. At the ripe old age of sixty, a widower with a grown son, one has certainly lived life to the full and one is well aware of its limitations. So, I was looking for a lady who would provide me the friendship and companionship I needed to meet both my public requirements and private inclination. I naturally assumed she would also be advanced in her age, either a widow or divorcee, it hardly mattered. Imagine my surprise and happiness when I found Mina. She was all I had ever dreamed of, after all a woman of her age, thirty-eight was hardly going to bother with an old fogey like me. But the well worn cliché, that age doesn't matter, seemed to apply to us very well. Because it didn't. Nothing did except a joyous meeting of the minds and an instant physical rapport. I am pleased to say that I seemed to satisfy her in that area extremely well.

I was marrying again after a gap of many years and was looking forward to it. My son, of course, did not see it the way I did. After I had informed him of my decision, his disapproval arrived in a week's time through the mail.

Mina and I had just finished dinner and were enjoying

our coffee. We were seated in the study room having decided that coffee needed to be taken in a more casual atmosphere than the ambience of the drawing and dining room. The room was small and cosy and exuded an informality that was not found elsewhere. The curtains were a warm beige silk that went beautifully with the vivid upholstery in an Aztec design. Colourful cushions were thrown everywhere even on the carpet which was again a muted shade of beige and orange. Since it was an easy room people invariably relaxed here finding great comfort in its warmth and simplicity.

'Dear dad' my son had written in an unusually neat hand. There was obviously no time for pleasantries for he went straight into it. 'I was extremely surprised to hear of your impending marriage to Mrs Mina Khanna. I hope you will be happy but I doubt it very much, indeed I fear for your happiness. Mina is a divorcee and if that is not cause to give her up then I do beg you to reconsider and think of the differences in your age. She is some twenty plus years younger than you, in fact hardly ten years older than me and you want her to be my new mama! If you cannot understand that the great disparity in your ages is cause for concern then at least think of her. She will be the subject of taunts and snide remarks as you will be. People will laugh behind your back and soon the whole of society in which you have such a high position will make fun of you. I beg you to reconsider, for such a match would prove disastrous for both you and your future relationship with me. I remain your devoted son, Ashwin.'

The formal tone of the letter infuriated me but more than that y son's narrowmindedness made me ashamed of him. I tossed the letter aside. There was no point in showing it to Mina. It would just upset her and I was hurt that my son, to whom I had given so much of myself after his mother died should be so uncaring of my happiness and more worried about what people would say.

I did, however, show it to Arundhati who did not fail me. As usual she said the right thing. I knew she would. She had this amazing ability to organise other people's lives.

After reading the letter, she gently folded it and gave it back to me. She then came and sat down next to me. "You have always been there for me when I needed you and always told me what was right and wrong. Do what your heart tells you, find happiness and don't waste your time in pettiness and trying to make others happy. Live for yourself." At the sweetness of her words and the relief I felt combined to make me behave in an extremely uncharacteristic fashion. I, a grown man of almost sixty, cried! Yes, can you believe it, I actually cried.

Apart from everything else, I realised that I was becoming older every passing day. In my youth I had never been the victim of self-doubt and self-pity. It was a stranger to me. I determined I was not going to give in to this vengeful stranger but do exactly what my heart told me to. After that I felt inordinately proud of myself and decided to never let this weakness of mine bother me again.

After the disappointing letter from my son, I let the situation lie low for a while. But although Ashwin had never met Mina, He had certainly heard about her, every chance I got to talk about her I did – I mentioned the movies we had been to; we were both keen movie buffs or the new restaurant we had just tried – but he either kept a cold silence and did not say anything or he would promptly change the subject. It was as if by not talking about her he could dismiss her out of our lives.

We were having a leisurely breakfast on Sunday after

both having played a round of golf. I was commenting on his late nights and he began to tell me about what a good time he had at the most recent night club, the Cabana, to join the ranks of the many that were appearing on the landscape. I listened to him with paternal pride and then began to tell him about my evening.

"You know this new restaurant that has just opened off Minto Road?" and as he nodded affirmation with his mouth full of bacon and eggs, I continued, "well, Mina and I decided to try it out last nig. . . ."

"Dad, I have to rush, I forgot I was supposed to meet one of my friends at the pool," and with a wave of his hand, he was gone.

It was always the same story but I was determined to stop this foolishness.

"Shekhar dear, do not be such a fool and stop pacing up and down like a frightened mouse," Arundhati said the morning I had fixed a meeting between the two for lunch. I had not told my son that Mina was joining us as well and was actually dreading the whole thing. I wished I could call it off but it was too late now.

"Arundhati, you know Ashwin, he refuses to even acknowledge her existence and now when I tell him we are going to be married, what's going to happen?" I was worried and tense, both people were precious parts of my life and it was important that they get on well together. The whole thing was snowballing and becoming a bigger and bigger disaster.

Why do children hold their parents to ransom so many times? Why does their approval or disapproval matter so much? I was a grown man who had been married before, had a grown son, seen my beloved wife die and yet here I was trembling like an old fool because I wanted my son's approval, I wanted him to say it was all right. Why did one give of oneself so much that another person holds the reins to your happiness?

It was even worse when they met. I had arranged a meeting at the Golf Club, a neutral place and one that all of us enjoyed going to. Secretly, I was hoping to avoid any unpleasantness and felt that he would hardly do or say anything acrimonious in such a public place. I was so happy that day thinking they would both love each other as much as I loved them. I admit I was nervous, more of my son's reactions than Mina's. After all, it is not every day that a father introduces his bride to be to his son. Also his letter had struck a sour note in our otherwise smooth relationship and I was keen that things get back to an even footing.

Mina was looking particularly beautiful that day in a peach sari. The only pieces of jewellery were the pearl and diamond drops and her engagement ring, both from me and I was delighted that she had chosen those two to wear. Her hair was flowing till her shoulders as I liked it and I must admit as I watched her walk towards us, I felt my heart bursting with pride and love.

I took her hand and turned towards my son. "Ashwin", I said more loudly than I intended, "meet my future wife Mina. Mina-Ashwin." They looked at each other. Mina tried to keep the warm smile on her face with difficulty while Ashwin just looked at her coldly. It was all his fault. He looked her up and down as if she was someone I'd picked off the roadside. To be fair to Mina, she tried to overlook his crass behaviour by talking to him amicably even though I could see she was upset.

"Your father talks about you all the time," she said to Ashwin and sat down on one of the chairs pulling me down with her. I saw Ashwin's lips tighten at this play of hands and he gave a nasty smirk which none of us could avoid seeing was deliberate. Mina is not one to be pushed around. She might be small and petite but underneath that soft exterior she can give as good as she gets. At this horrible display of Ashwin's she looked him full in the face and gave him back sneer for sneer. Then apologising to me for what she was going to say, she let Ashwin have it, head on.

"Shekhar, I am sorry I have to say this but I think I must. I was hoping we could all be good friends but now I can see that it is not meant to be. Your son has a lot of growing up to do. He should be happy that you have found someone to share your lonely life with but no, instead like a spoilt child, he wants to still hold on to his father's hand. He has a life of his own but he does not want you to have one." She turned towards Ashwin, "I am no fallen woman as you so delicately put it to your father in your letter. We happen to have found happiness together and we are going to go ahead and get married." I know she could have said a lot more but she controlled herself. She rose and said goodbye to both of us leaving Ashwin looking like he'd been hit with a bomb and me feeling ashamed of my son.

There was complete silence for a moment. I could see Shekhar indecisive and caught in the middle. But it was Ashwin I was looking at. The colour had drained from most of his face leaving a pink patch on his nose and cheeks. His lips were ground together and I could see he was on the verge of losing his cool. He did not want to antagonise his father, he was not stupid and knew where the money was coming from. He was staring at me but his brain was perceptibly darting from thought to thought as he wondered if he had gone too far.

I looked at him in disgust. My own son! Why, he was nothing but a wastrel. He was disgusting. I looked at the face which I thought was so like mine but I could see no resemblance. He was blabbing incoherently and made a pathetic sight. I felt for both of us.

As she hurried away, I followed her and tried to pacify her without making it too obvious to other people. I hated displays of this kind in public because it invariably was seen from a different perspective from someone or the other who knew you and then of course blown out of all proportion into a totally different story. When I got back, I paused for a moment from the door and watched my son as he yawned affectedly and made a great show of watching people walk to and from the bar with their drinks.

I wondered at this immature and boorish behaviour and was deeply saddened by what he had become. I had expected his support, love and friendship. Instead he had delivered me this terrible blow. We stared at each other in silence and I decided there was no mincing words. I had to tell him what I thought of him.

"You are a total disgrace to me. How on earth could you behave in that boorish manner? I expected so much more from you. I thought you would exult in my happiness but instead you behave like an immature school boy. I am ashamed of you and have no desire to call you my son."

He stared back at me insolently and then rising from the chair he was lounging in so indolently, he said, "Don't talk to me like that. I have every right to talk to anyone the way I want to. You are making a fool of yourself and can't see it. Well, I have tried to help you but I can see you are totally taken in by this . . . this tart."

For a moment there was a silence. Even he could see he had gone too far. "Do not talk about her like that," I shouted at him. I am normally a very placid sort of fellow but my son had riled me to the point of ridicule and there was no getting away from it. "Get out of my sight. Just go and never let me see your face again."

His face had turned a nasty grey-white and he had a pinched look about him. "Well," he said caustically with a bitter laugh, "it is obvious which side you have chosen and there is nothing I can do about it" and with a last long look he stormed out of the bar.

I was exhausted and slumped into the waiting armchair. I knew I had lost my son but I also knew that he had no right to be so judgemental. Mina and I were going to be married and that was all there was to it.

That night at dinner there was a long silence between us. I knew I must say something to ward off further unpleasantness. I told Ashwin as much. Mina and I were to be married. We would like him to be part of our future life but if he found he could not be a part of it then there was nothing further to be said. I loved him very much, that feeling would always be there and nobody could take his place but if he could not behave himself then there was nothing more to be said.

39

Nemesis, the dictionary tells us means something evil and bad. I do not know why but when I met Shekhar's son the word just occurred to me. He was the other side of the coin, the part of Shekhar that was not good.

Though he was as tall as his father, he had neither his presence or charisma. In a few minutes, I could see he was a trivial individual who had things too easy all his life. The only great thing about him was his greed which had mushroomed because his father had always given in to his demands. He thought everything was going just fine and then boom, I appeared on the scene. We hated each other on sight.

Ashwin had been thoroughly spoilt and Shekhar was totally to blame. After his wife died, he had concentrated so hard on looking after him and trying to fill the void that she had left that without really knowing it, or perhaps may be he did, he had given in to his every whim. In return he had grown up weak and wilful. He was indeed blessed with all the good things of life; youth, health, good looks and a doting father who saw that all his financial needs were met coupled with the sure knowledge that he was to inherit from his father all his wealth plus the good social position in society. Indeed, most of his friends thought he was a lucky rogue and before his father's announcement of marriage, he did indeed feel that he was.

Ashwin looked around at all the people having a good time. He could see his father was happy at his eventual recapitulation and surprisingly he felt happy too. He was glad he had seen sense and not become an impediment in his father's path to happiness.

My mother died when I was barely five and though as a child I would often cry and wonder why she had left me, I believed that I had been bad and thus was entirely to blame. By the time I had reached my teens these memories had all but disappeared and the truth was I hardly remembered her at all. Apart from my father upon whom I doted there was my father's sister, now deceased who had helped bring me up. She was a widow with no children and thus enjoyed the authority imposed on her. She was a strong woman with definite views and hardly any love to give. I hated her from the moment I set eyes on her and did not shed a tear when she died from a sudden heart attack. To be honest, I felt nothing at all and when I do think of her, if ever it is with utter indifference. But I always concealed my true feelings from my father for I knew he would be appalled if he knew the state of my mind. He being such a kind and generous person. That was ten years ago and I enjoyed just being with my father. I thought that was how it was always going to be. Till Mina stepped into the picture and spoilt everything.

I worshipped my father. He was a powerful looking man, extremely handsome with a strong physique and a personality to match. His very presence was soothing and all my life I had nothing to fear for I knew he would always be there for me. His very smile would envelop me in its warmth and make me feel as if I was ten feet tall. As I grew older, people would remark at the similarity between us and that would make me burn with pride. But while I knew we were physically alike, the same hazel eyes with long eyelashes, wide forehead and strong acquiline jaw. Clefts in both our chins which were square and strong and lips that were almost the same, though mine were thinner, in fact I was slightly taller than him, we were mentally poles apart. I knew he was truly one of those great individuals whom people would always admire. Where I was known because of him, I did not possess his strength of character and in a moment of dispassionate self-criticism, I knew I never would. I was mentally weak and spoilt. I had too much of the good life very early on and it had prevented me from forming any backbone, any reserves, for I knew I only had to ask and the deed would be done.

I loved my father unashamedly and would have done anything for him as long as it was not too strenuous but when he announced his intention of getting married, I could not face the situation. I felt he had betrayed me, after all were we not happy on our own? Why did he need another woman? He could take his pick of all the society women and there would be no need to legalise his position. I felt he was being a fool and told him so. I have never seen him look at me so coldly as he did on that day. That horrible scene with every terrible word has impaled itself on my mind.

Dad was waiting for me in the living room and had obviously been pacing about for some time.

"I am sorry to have kept you waiting, dad," I said. "I should have known you would be waiting for me on time for such an important meeting. I left work on time but you know how the traffic is . . . ." I was nervous and rambled on for a bit. ". . . . I swear it is getting worse every day. When will the country learn that we cannot continue like this forever? The government needs to take a good look at the country's infrastructure. We desperately need new roads, one way systems, flyovers, new parking lots. . . ."

Dad who was usually in complete command of every

situation I have ever seen him in, smiled nervously. I could see he was uneasy and I knew what I was about to say would hurt him deeply.

"Look Dad, you are an old man. I mean, I know you are in tremendous shape and I thank God for that but in terms of your actual age you could be called 'old." I don't mean any disrespect when I say this but you cannot honestly be serious about marrying this woman. It is not in good taste at all." He stared at me steadily. His face growing more and more still with every passing moment. I hurried on, struggling with my words, but still confident I was doing the right thing. "You are going to get nothing out of this marriage while this . . . this person has everything to gain."

Mina felt content and happy as she watched a couple gyrating on the dance floor oblivious to everything but themselves. A momentary shiver ran through her as she remembered those ugly scenes with Ashwin.

After that horrible episode, I actually thought about giving Shekhar up. He had stood there not saying a word. I could understand the trauma he was going through, the feeling of being caught in the middle but if he wanted to marry me surely he should have stood up to his son. Honestly, he was behaving abominably, after all it was his son!

Later on after my temper had cooled down and I had dried my tears of anger and indignation, I thought about the whole matter rationally. Where his emotions were concerned, Shekhar was slow to react. Once his mind was made up there was no holding him back but till then, well it was a slow journey. His relationship with his son was having to be redefined because he had allowed him to have the upper hand all these years and now that he wanted to be on an equal footing it was proving very awkward.

Apart from his son tugging at his parental emotions

his own feelings were in a state of disarray. In a way he had learned to live on his own preferring his own company to that of the too eager widows, desperate divorcees and even mothers with old unwed daughters. When he first met me, I admit despite my recent divorce and heartache, I had done the running. He was wary of giving in to his emotions believing it to be a temporary attraction and when he realised it was more than that he was scared, preferring to protect the single status he had held on to all these years. He was slow to perceive the enormous change fate had wrought for him but when he did, he held on tenaciously and I knew he would give up his son for me if necessary.

After the fiasco between Mina and my son, I tried to think rationally. Why was he behaving so abominably? After having devoted half my life to him surely I deserved some happiness of my own? He was being boorish and selfish and as much as I loved him, I loved Mina as well. I was looking forward to our life together and now that I had put to rest my personal fears about the disparity between our ages, I resolved to move forward.

Mina left for a week to the cooler climes of the hills in an attempt that both of us put the situation in perspective. I knew my mind, there would never be anyone but Mina. Still, I did not make any wedding plans, I thought that might tempt fate and prove catastrophic for me. I went through a painful period of another kind where I thought about her all the time but did not mention her name out loud in case some bad luck befall the future. In any case that did not prove too difficult, for apart from a few friends, no one really enquired after her.

On the day of her arrival, I was a nervous wreck and had exhausted myself with different imagined scenarios and thousands of different speeches. As my car drew up her driveway, my heart beat so loudly. I thought I might be having a heart attack. I got out of the car with difficulty, my legs no longer seemed to have the strength to carry me and my hands were all fingers and thumbs.

I was shown into the drawing room and had barely sat in the double armchair when she entered the room. We looked at each other at the same time and everything else became a blur.

I do not remember standing up, or her moving across the room. But suddenly she was in my arms and I was kissing her upturned face and salty tears. I found I was crying, Tears of joy and relief. She had come back to me and I vowed I would never let such a precious happiness be taken away from me.

"I had to come back, I just had to come back to you," she exclaimed passionately. "I love you so much, Shekhar. Please do not let your son's anger and hurt destroy what we have. I cannot and will not live without you."

I had not intended to talk about him at all other than to tell her of my decision. But she saw through his anger. She said it was a self-defence mechanism that acted as a shield against his hurt even though it was childish and totally unnecessary.

We discussed our wedding plans. I was no longer afraid to say those magic words, and we both decided we wanted a small wedding. I was relieved. I had thought that for her sake, I would put up with the usual showy affair but she immediately turned the idea down. "I want to marry you, Shekhar. The ceremony should have meaning for me. I am not putting on a display for other people. It is you I want . . ."

We were married two weeks later. It was quite a rush but neither of us wanted to wait. We had wasted so much time already it seemed every extra minute was important.

It was a small and dignified ceremony. An intensely personal affair in contrast to the lavish showing we could have gone in for. Certainly one that my status deserved according to most people. But most people weren't invited. Mina's parents, Arundhati, Avinash and their son along with Tara and Rohit were her invitees. The two people close to me were my mother-in-law and my son. So there were nine guests including the *pandit* who was also a close friend.

> Ashwin was laughing loudly at something his father had just said. They were both so tall and so very handsome. It was good to see them happy together. Tara and Mina looked at each other at that moment and both smiled. They remembered the confrontation they had with Ashwin.

Jealousy was no stranger to me and I could immediately recognise the symptoms when they overtook another. I told Mina about my suspicions and she agreed with me saying she suspected as much herself.

She then confronted Ashwin directly but true to her nature, she went headlong into the matter and threw caution to the winds. "It is plain to see that you are jealous of. . . ."

He never let her finish the sentence, "Jealous?" He looked stunned for a moment. "How dare you . . . you insinuate such a thing?" He drew himself to his full height and standing there so tall and so handsome but with the hurt face of a small child one couldn't help but feel sorry for him.

"Yes, jealous," repeated Mina. "Jealous, jealous, jealous. You are jealous of the affection your father gives me. Jealous that he might replace me in place of you."

He put on a look of disdain and shrugged his shoulders as if the whole conversation was beneath him. "What absolute rubbish. Why, why on earth would I be jealous of someone like *you?*" The look he gave me was withering and filled with scorn.

"I will always be my father's son and despite your best effort nothing you can do can displace his affection for me."

I could see Mina was both hurt and angry but controlling herself with visible difficulty she said, "Look I have absolutely no need to try and worm my way into your father's affections as you insinuate. He loves me but he loves you too, and will always love you. Surely you cannot be so selfish as to deny your father the right to love again, find happiness with another woman?"

He looked miserable. "Why, why does he need to have anyone else, we've lived for so many years without anyone except each other? Why now does he suddenly decide he needs you? What's so special about you any way?"

It was more than I could stomach. "What do you mean 'what's so special about me?' What's so special about you? Why should an attractive man of your father's age deny himself the obvious happiness he is getting out of being with me for an overgrown, selfish and boorish person like you? You might be his son, but what right do you have to hold his emotions to ransom? What have you ever done in your life but think about yourself and your needs? Did you ever pause to think what your father might want? He has given up so much for you and still it is not enough. What more do you want?"

Mina was trembling with fury and turned away in disgust. She walked away and then turned back. "Your father is going to marry me irrespective of anything else, but it will pain him that you cannot be part of his decision. You already have so much, why don't you for once do something for him?"

We did not except this confrontation to amount to anything. But then a few days later, he arrived at my doorstep.

"Look Mina . . ." I was uncomfortable in this new role that consisted solely of penance and paused realising the delicacy of the moment. Mina could see something was troubling me but her stony face showed no flicker of emotion at my obvious discomfort.

"Look Mina, I was mistaken about you. For a long time I have stood in the way of dad's and your happiness. At first I thought you were a short-term distraction but as both of you became closer to each other, I started to panic. I have rather selfishly thought I should be the only recipient of dad's love. I am sorry for the pain I have caused you and hope you will both forgive me in time."

I was filled with a feeling of great and overwhelming happiness. And standing on tiptoe, I kissed him on his cheek.

So the ice had been broken and over the next few days we even managed to be civil to each other. By the time of the wedding he seemed to have lost most of his animosity and I was only thankful that it had happened just in time. Shekhar was beside himself with joy and continually pulled us together for pictures of his "two favourite people."

Mina saw Arundhati and Tara I the garden. She had enough of chatting with other people and she moved towards her two dearest friends.

The evening had been dusty and humid. The wind tore through the grass and flowers, scattering them in all directions. It howled and screamed and looked like it was an all night party. But abruptly its ferocity was cut short by the sudden arrival of rain. It took over and refused to leave. All night it poured incessantly unmindful of the twigs that broke from the trees, the overripe fruits that fell in abundance splaying their contents all over the ground or the incandescent hibiscus and white jasmine that were no match against the onslaught and were ruthlessly torn from their shelter.

40

It was the early hours of the morning and the party showed no signs of ending. The room reeked of stale smoke and heavy perfumes. There was a lot of raucous laughter, music that had turned more seductive and people no longer clung to their inhibitions but seemed more carefree and spoke with wild abandon.

Arundhati was impervious to her surroundings. She sat alone on the terrace unnoticed but with a clear view of the many scenes being enacted inside. The wine she had drunk had coursed through her veins leaving her mellow and introspective. But her thoughts came to her with crystal clarity.

She thought of the three of them – Tara, Mina and herself. What good friends they had become. Adversity had thrown them together and each had shared and learnt from the other's experience. They had been thrown into the fast flowing waters with no means of survival at hand and yet they had overcome their almost certain fate and grasped whatever means to emerge alive and victorious.

They were each different women. Of all the three, she had started life out with the most and also lost a lot.

Arundhati was an idealist, a dreamer, a solitary person who always stood somewhat apart, on the fringe of life. Such a person lives more for his dreams than in actuality and when she was pushed into living, she found herself completely betrayed. Her womanhood had been rejected and her dreams destroyed. But she had won a small victory – her son. He was no consolation price, indeed she never saw him as an alternative to what could have been. He had his place in her heart. Still, life must leave an effect of the ravages. There was an emptiness about her that was new, a certain ambiguity that could not be reached but there was also a glimmer of hope that still flickered faintly. . . .

Tara born and raised in a different environment had spent much of her childhood desperate for love. The need to be shown affection had been denied by her mother and she replaced it with an almost manic need not to be like her mother. This almost ferocious resolve wreacked its own havoc. She denied her true self and almost lost all that she had worked hard for but through sheer courage and a well nurtured resilience she overcame her loss and turned it into success.

Mina was a cross between the two of them. She had seen life at closer quarters, worked hard for a living fuelled by a determination and ambitions to make something of herself. In this aspect she was close to Tara who also had great ambition albeit the goals were different. Her survival did not come with less pain rather the hurt healed with the help of great love. Of the three, she was perhaps the happiest.

We have each trod the path fate set in store for us, looked for alternatives and on finding it unsuitable, finally after much anguish and torment written our own lines, forged new destinies. We have given of ourselves unstintingly only to be dealt out by life's largesse. So we dried our tears refusing to let them fall again, hid the bruises that pained our bodies and the welts that hurt long after the flesh had mended and straightened our backs bent with suffering to walk upright again. The dream of our youth still as vivid as ever brought back from some deep recess to burn ever more brightly as it lit a flame, discovering a new path that had long remained hidden from our vision.

For the three of them many things had changed. Life had taken then through some strange and painful events that none of them could have forseen. They were older and perhaps wiser letting go of memories fermented by constant unhappiness, while allowing new happenings to enter without prejudice and mingle with the good and the new.

41

At first, there were a few drops of rain scattering now and again in a desultory manner. We had almost got used to the lethargic drizzle the way one puts up with a crochety old aunt; you make the best of it. But with a suddenness, that brought us out of our complacency, the clouds shattered the skies with thunder and the drops of rain became a torrent.

The winds howl with companionable alacrity and when they both join forces, we find ourselves unwilling prisoners. We shut the windows tightly and bolt the doors but that is no match for them for they sneak in through the crevices, the loose tiles and stained glass. They entwine us from within shaking a bolt free and slamming against the door. These inanimate objects are no match against their joint onslaught and very soon they have reached the threshold. They move brazenly flaunting their power and before our very eyes they emerge the victor, howling with a passion that is life itself.